Testimonials

Astronaut Edgar Mitchell, Ph.D. *(Sixth man to walk on the moon):* "*I am an American astronaut and a trained scientist. Because of my position people in high places confide in me. And, as a result, I have no doubt that aliens HAVE visited this planet. The American government and governments throughout the world have thousands of files of UFO sightings which cannot be explained. The stories I have heard from these people, who are more highly qualified than me to talk about UFOs, leave me in no doubt that aliens have already visited Earth...*"

Stanton Friedman. Nuclear Physicist: "*The evidence is overwhelming that Planet Earth is being visited by intelligently controlled extraterrestrial spacecraft.*"

Dr. Steven Greer, The Disclosure Project: *On Wednesday, May 9th, 2001, over twenty military, intelligence, government, corporate and scientific witnesses came forward at the National Press Club in Washington, DC to establish the reality of UFOs or extraterrestrial vehicles, extraterrestrial life forms, and resulting advanced energy and propulsion technologies. The weight of this first-hand testimony, along with supporting government documentation and other evidence, will establish without any doubt the reality of these phenomena.*

Charles J. Camarda (Ph.D.) *NASA Astronaut:* "*In my official status, I cannot comment on ET contact. However, personally, I can assure you, we are not alone!*"

Monsignor Corrado Balducci, a Vatican theologian, said: *"Extraterrestrial contact is a real phenomenon. The Vatican is receiving much information about extraterrestrials and their contacts with humans from its embassies in various countries, such as Mexico, Chile and Venezuela."*

Professor Stephen Hawking: *"Of course it is possible that UFO's really do contain aliens as many people believe, and the Government is hushing it up."*

Ben Rich, second director of Lockheed Skunkwork's from 1975-1991: *"There are two types of UFOs — the ones we build and the ones 'they' build."*

Mikhail Gorbachev, the USSR's last head of state: *"The phenomenon of UFOs does exist, and it must be treated seriously."*

CHOSEN

Bethany's Story

by

Louise Rose Aveni

Angel House Publishing

Disclaimer

This book was written as a work of fiction and, as such, any resemblance to persons living or dead is strictly the result of intertwining a compilation of personalities with the author's artistic creativity.

Cover design by Debi DeSantis Stabene

Interior design by Audria Wooster and Louise Rose Aveni

ISBN: 978-0-9675124-4-0

Angel House Publishing, Sarasota, Florida

Printed in the U.S.A. 2019

Table of Contents

Dedication

I lovingly dedicate this book to my eldest daughter, Christine, who was a major catalyst for my writing this spin-off novel to the HYBRID-The Trilogy saga. Her insistence to know more about Bethany, a five-year old, high-level psychic who interacted with hybrids, inspired me to create the backstory and what happened to this most intriguing character.

And so, for you Christine... here she is!

Author's Note

When I wrote LUPO - Conversations with an E.T., which is the first of three stories in the HYBRID saga, it was my intention to create a captivating story that would put a non-threatening face and voice to those benevolent beings who have walked among us for millennium and who may, in fact, BE dominant in humanity's very creation.

The main character, Stephan, is loosely cast after a real person, a well-respected business owner I became friendly with while living in Boca Raton, Florida. This unassuming man, candidly shared his amazing early life as a young orphan in Italy and spoke convincingly of his nightly visitations and sojourns with E.T.s and how his own high level of psychic abilities have altered his earthly journey ever since.

So intriguing was his story, that I expressed it would make a terrific book and how I would like to be the one to write it!

He agreed with two stipulations; first, it must be written as a book of fiction for both his protection and mine; and the second caveat was that I must promise to never reveal his identity, for he IS a hybrid. A promise I have kept to this day.

And so, I artistically wove a tapestry of Faction (a term I mused as part fact, part fiction), constructed from his unique life recitations, coupled with some of my personal unearthly happenings while living in Sedona, Arizona; then added accounts from others who had shared their own experiences of contact and encounters with off planet beings and interdimensional entities. The result – HYBRID- The Trilogy!

It was my hope that HYBRID would provide a key to open skeptical minds to not only consider the possibilities of life on other planets and interdimensional beings but embrace the plausibility and probability that some of these people and events are, indeed, factual and not simply the product this author's inspired imagination, or merely some anecdotal stories from mythology-based thinkers.

I then had to research, in earnest, the government's long held Truth Embargo relative to the E.T. presence and what their covert role was in this global suppression of full disclosure regarding the U.F.O. phenomenon.

Thankfully today, more than ever, trace evidence, credible witness testimony, a plethora of video footage, along with the declassification of volumes of secret U.F.O. files from multiple governments around the globe, has unleashed and exposed the extreme degree of illegal, covert operations at the core of this U.F.O. and E.T. secrecy.

Believing I had had told the story I wished to tell, I thought I was done, but apparently, not so. For what I found was a flood of questions from my readers about one character in particular, who had won their hearts and devoured their curiosity about wanting to know more about her, how she came to be and what happened to her next.

That character is a high-spirited, precocious five-year old named Bethany, an extremely elevated psychic whose was chosen to teach young interdimensional hybrids how to interact with humanoids in an effort to walk among them undetected. Her unabashed approach to life reminded the reader to remain open and re-engage the child in us all to consider the possibilities... then watch what happens!

So, without further ado, I give you **Chosen – Bethany's Story.**

Prologue

Washington, D.C., October 1964, approximately 5:00 a.m. EST; somewhere under the White House, in one of many dark, barely lit, catacomb tunnels that covertly take those who wish to go unnoticed to destinations of the highest secrecy, something extraordinary, is occurring. A dubious, surreptitious protocol that the majority of American citizens have only heard conspiratorial stories about but never truly considered its validity.

The private chartered bus, bleak in color with no visible markings, or even a license plate, maneuvers the tunnel's narrow roadway, illuminated only by soft amber circular reflectors strategically positioned on either side of the cavernous walls so as to provide adequate guideposts to the driver.

The road surface, while paved, is still rudimentary and uneven; most likely a result of the frequent military heavy transport equipment that also utilizes this clandestine highway.

The driver, a middle aged, somewhat overweight male, dressed all in black, wipes the moist droplets of sweat that have begun to form on his furrowed brow. He squints his barely awake eyes that strain to maintain his fuzzy interpretation of what should be a familiar trek. After all, he's taken this sojourn more times than he can count.

His concentration is momentarily diverted by the crackling voice that emits from his two-way walkie-talkie that's conveniently mounted on the vehicle's dashboard for easy access. The driver reaches for the radio and quietly utters, "Murphy here. What's up? Over."

The radio crackles again as the voice on the other end inquires, "Where are you? What's your ETA? Over." The driver responds, "I'm about thirty minutes out. Over."

The other voice continues, "And the cargo? Over." The driver responds, "All sleeping. Wish I was. Over." The voice answers, "10-4. Copy that. Over." Placing the walkie-talkie back into its cradle, the driver quickly checks his interior rearview mirror to ensure his passengers remain in their silent repose. They are.

Not long afterwards, the driver brings the bus to a slow stop, then sits immobile before a dead-end portion of the road that faces a solid cement wall. He stares patiently at the barrier before him knowing that, within seconds, it will spread open just wide enough to accommodate the vehicle's girth. Right on cue, the wall rumbles as the mechanical device strains to move this mountain of rock, allowing the bus to exit from its hollow abyss and enter onto a well-lit portion of a deserted highway.

It's now approaching 7:00 a.m. EST and the only evidence of the traveling troops' location is a large green and white sign that illuminates from the vehicle's headlights; it reads - *Welcome to West Virginia.*

The next hour passes uneventfully as the dawn's early light begins to fill the interior of this transporter of precious cargo. One by one the small occupants begin to stir fitfully. As their mildly sedated bodies begin to shake off the induced effects, a small voice croaks from the interior, "Are we there yet?" To which the driver mumbles with a smirk, "Almost", then laughs to himself at the normality of the question that seems universal with all kids who travel...however, this journey is anything but normal.

The bus makes a right turn off the main road onto a narrow dirt path that leads to its final destination - an isolated ranch that boasts a large cement building with no windows, which seems totally out of place in such a rural setting.

All twenty-seven of the young occupants, boys and girls ranging from age four up to twelve, are now fully awake and alert and begin to chatter loudly to one another as they excitedly anticipate getting off the bus.

The driver reminds himself that this unusual cargo will soon be out of his charge, as they disembark and are handed off to someone else. No longer his responsibility.

Early or not, it's time for a large, cold beer and a double cheeseburger, then his next task is to find himself a suitable place to lay his tired bones and rest before the return voyage, which will commence in approximately six hours.

The door of the bus hisses open and within seconds, two young women clad in plain khaki shirts and pants board the front of the bus and announce to the children to gather all their belongings, backpacks, jackets, sweatshirts, etc. and to follow them. The driver quips, "They're all yours!" as he too, steps off the bus, reaching into his top left-hand shirt pocket which holds the nicotine treasure he's long awaited to draw into his lungs, lo' these long hours.

One by one the children gingerly step off the bus, waving their hands in the air in disgust as they waft through the billowing cigarette smoke that is being exhaled from the driver's mouth.

The children step in line, like ducklings following their mother as they process to the cement building, bookended by the two women who silently take their charges to their purpose.

They momentarily halt in front of a door as the lead woman enters a numerical code into the weather worn keypad adjacent to the door. A small red light, changes to green, indicating entry is now possible.

The children follow the leader down a long sterile hallway, their voices somewhat subdued now. They arrive at yet another door with the same type of keypad that also displays the red light, prohibiting entry until the code is entered, then, as before, green appears– GO!

The children excitedly explode through this last doorway, giggling and shouting inaudible messages to those who have been patiently awaiting their arrival.

There before them stands thirty or so small, thin figures with disproportionately long arms with oversized heads; their large black, almond shaped, expressionless eyes staring back at them.

The room's interior is surprisingly flamboyant, filled with colorful murals of blue skies with white billowing clouds, fields of vibrant flowers and image after image of animal species from all over the world. The lower portion of the room's interior is cluttered with large industrial sized crates randomly placed on the non-descriptive indoor/outdoor carpeting; these containers overflow with every type of toy ever made, from simple building blocks to sophisticated, futuristic digital devices. This is indeed, a child's dream play house!

Within moments, the hysteria subsides as both the human children and the young alien hybrids assume their assigned positions at any one of the numerous small, round, colored plastic tables with matching plastic chairs. A voice from the P.A. system announces, in a robotic, monotone, "Now, you may begin."

BETHANY

*T*o most of the world, I am known as Bethany...Bethany Anne...(Anne with an 'e') Wilcox and I was born on February 10, 1994...however, to those inhabiting the dark underworld of governmental covert operations, otherwise referred to as the Black Ops, my identity is simply HF12765. The HF stands for "Human Female"; numerically, I am the twelve thousandth, seven hundred and sixty-fifth humanoid child in The Program to date...but even that's an ever-increasing number.

The Program? The easiest way to explain that one is to simply state that in the aftermath of the renowned 1947 Roswell, New Mexico UFO incident, the age-old question that arose "Are they here?" was no longer part of the equation. Rather it became, "Why are they here?" and which government will stand in good stead with these highly advanced Star Beings with the ultimate goal being to secure and maintain control of the planet and its riches - The Ultimate Power!

I know, I know, hard to swallow any of this, right? So, if I may, let me enlighten you with a bit of not so well- known U.S. History. Here goes.

Around 1978, U.S. intelligence sources, along with other secretive agencies (not all originating from our plant), began "recruiting" (not always voluntarily, I might add) high level child psychics as part of an experiment; a galactic co-operative of sorts, with the end goal being to teach alien hybrids the ways of the human world in an effort to provide adequate cloaking, so they may walk among us undetected. At least that was the concept.

Initially called the Stargate Project, the objective was to investigate and pursue the potential to expand what was already

1

in place known as "remote viewing", which is the practice of seeking impressions about a distant or unseen target, purportedly using extrasensory perception (ESP) or "sensing" with the mind. This protocol was widely utilized by the military and other government task forces. But now, after decades working with off planet entities in exchange for their advanced technologies, the governments of the world engaged in yet another competitive agenda... who could successfully interact with these inter-stellar and inter-dimensional beings in an unremitting partnership to control the planet and its inhabitants? The gauntlet had been thrown down in earnest.

Me? I was one of the "chosen" to be part of that program, ready or not; for I AM a high-level psychic...their label, not mine. But I'm getting a bit ahead of myself. Let me explain...

Like I said, my name is Bethany Anne Wilcox, and I am the middle child and only girl born to my parents, Rachel and Lawrence (Larry) Wilcox. I have an older half-brother, Charlie, seven years my senior, who is the product of my Mom's teenage...um...let's see, how did her side of the family describe it?... oh yeah... "indiscretion." Don't get me wrong, Charlie is dearly loved by both sides of the family and the total epitome of a loving, protective big brother. I adore Charlie...we remain extremely close, to this day.

I also have another sibling, Ryan, who is only a year and a half my junior and with whom I share many things besides our genetic DNA. For it appears that he, like me, has inherited the psychic gene. Etiology unknown. But more on that later.

I adore both my parents. Mom is such an amazing nurturer and one of my biggest cheerleaders in life, but I must admit to being somewhat of a "Daddy's girl", all the same. My Dad is so full of life; he can be stern and intimidating at times and yet he has this comedic side that will burst forth unexpectedly that keeps the family happily off balance.

I have always had the ability to know things and, unfortunately, feel physical and emotional experiences from other people. That's another label I own, for I am what is known as an empath.

Want to hear something weird? I was fully conscious while in the womb! While kids aren't aware of their environment until after birth, I was fully cognizant of my surroundings, sights and sounds in vitro. Here's another crazy fact, I have total recall and can recount the moment of my birth and everything thereafter. To this day, I can tell you the events of my life, thus far, to include the minutest details such as conversations that were exchanged and who was wearing what. I know...it's a lot to absorb, but nonetheless...this is ME!

So, here I am, a high-level psychic, and empath and I have total recall. I believe that's what's known as a triple threat. Lucky me!

And yet, for the most part, I considered myself to be a very happy, normal (my kind of normal, anyway) child. I have lots of fond memories of my earlier years. I was an energetic, albeit precocious kid, who never simply walked into a room...I exploded into a room, usually chattering all the way about one thing or another. I seemed to be the chief source of my family's entertainment in that I was always dancing and singing, demanding them to stop what they were doing, sit down and watch my latest performance, to which they lovingly obliged. Bless 'em.

I also have this uncanny ability to absorb new things at warp speed, which annoys others to no end. Case in point; my brother Charlie, who was eleven at the time, was taking piano lessons, (under great protest, I might add). As a compromise, my parents agreed to hire a private piano teacher who'd come to our home, once a week, late in the afternoon, so Charlie could still engage in after school sports, his truer passion. More importantly, (who's kidding who) so none of his buddies would know about this untapped talent and pounce on this buffet of an opportunity to humiliate him whenever they could. Boys!

At any rate, every week Charlie would sit begrudgingly before the upright piano my mother received as a gift from my dad, and awkwardly fumbled his fat fingers across the ivories in an attempt to plunk out the lesson of the day. Poor Charlie, his hands were designed to hold a football, not delicately caress the black and ivory keys.

One day, after Charlie's torturous lesson was finally over, my Mom led the piano teacher to the front door, while the teacher chattered in support of how, in time, Charlie would begin to embrace the beauty of this melodious instrument. (Yeah… sure.)

So now, enters little precocious four-year old me; who takes it upon myself to climb up onto the piano bench and place my tiny digits upon the keys. I began to play, (artfully I might add), the lesson that brother Charles has just mangled moments before. Both my Mom and the piano teacher's heads spun around, mouths agape as I played the short sonata, fait accompli!

"I think we're giving lessons to the wrong child!", the piano teacher cajoled. Thus, began my own test of will with this teacher, as it became abundantly clear to all that I preferred to play by ear, rather than learn the rudimentary mechanics of piano playing. End of lessons…for both Charlie and me.

But you know what? I didn't get that what I did was anything unusual or special because I believed everyone else was the same as me. But I was soon to discover differently and how quickly that belief changed.

(Flashback)

Springtime in Falls Church is definitely Bethany's favorite time of the year. Everything is bursting alive with a plethora of flowering Kousa Dogwood trees, Crape Myrtles, along with the luscious Magnolia and Cherry trees that speckle the neighborhood landscape with their vibrant hues and delicious fragrances.

But her all-time favorites are the tiny yellow and orange jonquils, purple crocuses and golden forsythia that line the burgeoning gardens surrounding her modest brick faced colonial home, framed with picture perfect pure white shutters.

These are the meek pleasures of nature that delight a five-year old, whose only mission in life, thus far, is to simply BE! Even the birds seem to be singing more in earnest as they herald the first light of this new day in the small Virginian urban village.

But in vast contrast of all this exterior beauty, inside the bedroom she shares with her three and a half - year old brother, Ryan, Bethany is fitfully awaking and softly begins to moan and whimper as she tosses and turns beneath her quilted coverlet. Ryan, who has been awake for some time, is amusing himself on the floor next to his bed with his Fisher -Price Musical Lullaby TV that repeatedly plays "Row, Row, Row, Your Boat" and "London Bridge" in succession, somewhat ignoring his older sister's seeming distress.

Bethany twists and convulses in earnest now, as if in serious pain, then suddenly bolts upright, throwing off her bed covers. Placing her tiny hands over her ears, eyes still shut tightly, she then begins to sing in unison with Ryan's musical toy...

"Row, row, row your boat, gently down the stream...merrily, merrily, merrily, merrily, life is but a dream."

Repeating the musical phrasing over and over, her voice getting louder and louder with each echoed verse until she finally stops in mid song, releases her hands from her ears, takes in a deep breath and then whispers, "There… it's gone. All gone, Ry. Ry… All gone…", her voice trails off.

Ryan hesitantly puts down his toy. The room is now eerily silent, as the two siblings exchange an unspoken glance; eyes locked in momentary trance. It is Ryan who breaks the spell, as he swiftly pads his way over to his sister's side; all the while stealthily stepping over the toys and books that are randomly strewn about the carpeted floor, hoping he doesn't ding one of his little toes en route.

Leaning in on his elbows, closed fists supporting his chin, he offers one of his million-dollar grins, bringing the pair fully back to the feeling of comfort and safety of their home.

Their reverie is short lived as their mother's voice calls from the floor below, "Come on you two lazy bones…time to get up… breakfast is ready! Who wants pancakes?"

Eyes popping wide open, the duo race through the bedroom door, almost tripping over one another as they battle for first position for the delicacies that await. Hearing the commotion from the floor above, mother Rachel giggles out loud while cautioning her children to be careful as they thump down the staircase to their destination…the kitchen.

Pre-teen Charlie, eldest of the trio, is already seated at the breakfast table, fully dressed and ready for school. Before him sits the piece de resistance, a full stack of hot buttery blueberry pancakes, piled high and is deftly deliberate in his administration of the final topping, gobs of gooey, amber colored, warm, maple syrup.

"Where's Dad?" Charlie asks, while pouring himself a hefty glass of ice-cold milk. "He had to be in work early, again, but with any luck he may be able to actually come home early",

Rachel wistfully answers with a sigh, while she delivers Ryan's pancakes at his place setting.

As primary bread-winner, Larry, has been putting in extra, long hours at the CPA firm he works for but that's of no surprise seeing whereas it's tax season. Larry has been with the firm for over seven years and is next in line for a promotion with promise of a substantial pay increase - so patience is the order of the day for the Wilcox household.

When the two younger children finally make their way into the kitchen, Ryan simply can't resist the overwhelming temptation to insert his index finger into the center of Charlie's delectable dish. In warp speed, Ryan extracts the small digit that now drips of the sugary delight, then shoves it into his tiny mouth, all the while smacking his now sticky maple syrupy lips. "Come on you little twerp", Charlie scolds, "Go eat your own… MOM!"

Rachel feigns a stern warning, subduing the snicker that awaits inside and lightly scolds, "That's enough Ry, Ry…here's yours." Bethany, who normally erupts into the morning scene, demurely takes her place at the family table then shoots a questioning glance at her mother, who responds, "Hang on, young lady, hang on…yours are coming."

Charlie unabashedly dotes on Bethany and likes to affectionately tease her when an opportunity presents itself. He's also been known to create that prospect, just for fun and for his personal entertainment. However, this particular morning, Charlie's distracted just enough and never questions his sister's subdued manner, which has replaced her ever present in your face deportment and so simply leaves her well enough alone.

With all children now seated and served, Rachel leans against the kitchen sink, both hands about her coffee mug, its contents now tepid and smiles, lovingly surveying her brood as they partake in their morning ritual.

The enchantment is broken with the sound of chair legs scratching the floor's surface as Charlie pushes back his wooden seat, then bolts upright, chattering about how he's going to miss his bus if he doesn't leave now!

With a quick, barely there, brush of a kiss on his mother's cheek, Charlie grabs his backpack that's slung over the back of his chair, while his other arm reaches for the half -full glass of milk on the table. Chugging its remains, he spins around to race out the kitchen door, mumbling what can only be surmised as a good-bye to his siblings. Gone!

"Oh boy!" Rachel sighs, as the last vibration of the slamming back door reverberates throughout the kitchen. "So, what would you two like to do today? I have some work to do in the garden...anyone want to help?" "I will! I will!" the children answer in excited chorus. "OK then, let's clean up the dishes and get you both dressed...but not before you brush your teeth", Rachel commands, which is met with a unanimous groan.

In no time at all the trio retreats to the small, well-trimmed backyard, complete with distressed wooden sand box, metal swing set and slide, whose painted exterior shows signs of wear and weather. Rachel and Ryan go about getting the gardening tools out of the small metal shed that sits adjacent to the sand box, while Bethany meticulously scouts out the bloomed flower beds, determining which ones she wants to pick. For she has a deliberate mission, therefore the choices she makes are paramount to her decision making.

Rachel and Ryan busy themselves digging holes for the new plantings that were just purchased over the weekend. Bethany walks about the various gardens, carefully selecting the best of the best for this very special bouquet. She softly mumbles words of thanks to each bloom for their contribution prior to picking them ...then smiles.

When she's chosen the perfect spay of assorted blossoms, Bethany runs to her mother's side in an unabashed display of pride, showing off her selections. As her little fingers fumble and struggle to hold them all, Rachel reaches for the pretty blue elastic Scrungie that holds Bethany's soft golden-brown curls away from her face, then gingerly wraps it about the blooms. "There!", Rachel declares, "How's that?" In full approval, Bethany can't contain the full-on grin that emits from her Cupie Doll lips.

"By the way, what do you plan to do with those flowers?" Rachel inquires. Bethany shoots a quick glance to Ryan before answering her mother, then declares boldly, "I'm going to give them to Mrs. Blanchard...to help her feel better." Mrs. Blanchard and her husband have been in the neighborhood for decades and are viewed as pseudo grandparents by the kids in the area due to their advancing age; which, in reality, puts them only in their late fifties, but to young children, that's ancient.

"I didn't know she was sick...that's very nice of you, sweetie", Rachel states as she turns her focus back to the planting, oblivious to the unspoken dialogue that's going on between Ryan and Bethany...a dialog that is usually reserved between twins...or in this case "gifted" children.

Ever since Bethany was born, she would display certain traits that were most puzzling to Rachel but more disconcerting to Larry. Frequently, Bethany would make random declarations about people she barely knew and told of events that were going to happen, some quite dark and disturbing in nature. Both Larry and Rachel questioned where the heck she was getting this stuff, especially since both Bethany and Ryan were cloistered from watching TV programs or movies that depicted violence or were laden with negative themes. So, it was distressing, to say the least, when Bethany would nonchalantly make these pronouncements about things that little children shouldn't know anything about.

It was Bethany who told her parents that another baby was coming into the family soon, that it would be a boy and his name was Ryan. Well, of course it all came to pass, and so they conceded (more likely in an attempt to appease a very insistent Bethany) and, indeed, named the new arrival, Ryan.

Right from the beginning, Bethany and Ryan had a special bond, one that defied most sibling ties. If one got sick, the other felt the same symptoms, albeit no trace of the same illness was medically present. It was easily dismissed and assumed they were simply mimicking the other as a form of solidarity or perhaps even attention getting. However, even when they were geographically separated, they knew exactly what was going on with the other, which was an unexplainable occurrence.

So, here they stood in the family garden, doing what they do, communicating like no others do, except them.

Once the trance is broken, Bethany asks if it's okay for her to bring the flowers over to Mrs. Blanchard and, oh by the way, "Ryan wants to come too." Rachel gives her permission but stresses that they're not to go into Mrs. Blanchard's home, especially with the possibility that she may be contagious.

Hand in hand, the two small children trek through their yard, past the aging swing set and then tunnel though the tall forsythia bushes, ablaze with their bountiful yellow blossoms, ever so careful to not get scratched from their wooden stems. Rachel stops her gardening long enough to watch her children as they march their way across the yard on their errand of kindness and compassion and feels proud of the thoughtful individuals they are becoming.

When they reach their destination, Bethany gently knocks on their neighbor's back door. At first no one answers. At Rachel's urging from her own yard, she tells Bethany to ring the bell, if she can reach it. Bethany stands on tippy-toe and does so with confidence and within moments Mrs. Blanchard cheerfully greets her visitors; eyeing the bouquet of freshly cut blossoms which she artfully deduces is the purpose of their unexpected visit.

"Well, thank you Bethany and Ryan. How very sweet of you both. Would you like to come in?", Mrs. Blanchard offers while waving a greeting to Rachel from across the yard.

"No thank you, Mrs. Blanchard. We're helping Mommy in the garden..." Bethany hesitates, then continues. "We wanted you to have these flowers...so you won't be sad...now that Mr. Blanchard is gone...but he's in heaven now...so don't be sad."

Not knowing how to respond to this, the confused neighbor tries to clarify, "Oh no, honey, Mr. Blanchard isn't in heaven. He's at work and, in fact, will be home in a few hours. Why would you think that?"

In her youthful candor, Bethany simply explains how she *saw* Mr. Blanchard in a church; "...but he was in a box with a white sheet over it and flowers on top and how the people were crying." The neighbor again states where Mr. Blanchard is and dismisses the unnerving declaration as this sweet child must have had a bad dream that seemed real to her.

Her mood now pensive, Mrs. Blanchard thanks the children again for the lovely flowers and sends them on their way, back to their mother and their own yard. Flowers in hand, shaking her head in wonderment, she closes the door, determined to put the strange motive for the visit out of her head.

When the children return to their mother, she tells them that what they did was a very nice thing, never realizing the dismal message that accompanied their thoughtful gesture. It's now time for lunch so they move inside, wash their hands and prepare to eat their mid-day meal.

Ryan and Bethany remain uncharacteristically quiet throughout lunch, so Rachel decides that a nap is in order to restore their routinely good nature.

Allowing the children to bed down in the living room, Rachel places one of their favorite DVD's into the player, with the hopeful intention of them relaxing enough to drift off into a peaceful rest. In no time at all, that's exactly what happens.

An hour passes; children are sleeping soundly. Rachel is actually able to put her own feet up for a bit before it's time to entertain the children, once again. Reclining her weary body on the Laz-Z-Boy that her husband Larry, more than not, inhabits when he's home, Rachel also easily drifts off into a light sleep.

A short time later, the ringing of the phone brings Rachel out of her respite. "Hello? Wait...what? Hold on...slow down...w-w-what happened? Oh my god! Yes, yes of course - whatever she needs...let me know." Rachel sits dumbfounded at the news she's just received.

The caller is a friend and neighbor, who lives just a few doors down from the Blanchards. She's calling to report that Mr. Blanchard was killed in a freak automobile accident this morning on his way to work. He died instantly. Mrs. Blanchard wasn't notified right away about her husband's passing due to a computer glitch when searching the database on the license plate. The identification process took even longer because Mr. Blanchard had inadvertently left his wallet that held his license at home, something he's never done before.

But just as shocking to Rachel was the claim by the neighbor that apparently Bethany told Mrs. Blanchard that she was sorry about Mr. Blanchard being in heaven and not to be so sad. "Wait a minute...what did you say?... Bethany said... w—w-what?"

Rachel grabs for the edge of the chair in an effort to catch her balance as the room begins to spin, all the while desperately trying to recall the chronology of events as they unfolded this morning with the children's visit to Mrs. Blanchard. But in truth, does any of this matter... because Bethany knew this before it happened. But how?

"Oh God, not again!", Rachel speaks aloud. For this wasn't the first time Bethany shocked people with her predictions. It had been a while since anything like this has happened and, quite frankly, she was hoping the previous incidents were just flukes...apparently not. But why? Why would Bethany even tell Mrs. Blanchard such devastating news and *WHY* didn't she tell me first? Rachel torments.

Rachel's shock quickly grows into anger. Without thinking, she rushes over to a sleeping Bethany, kneels beside her and begins yelling at her groggy child, while pounding her fist onto the carpeted floor. "Why do you do these things? Don't you realize that these things hurt people? I don't know where you're getting this stuff but it's got to stop! Do you hear me, Bethany? It's going to STOP!" her voice now hysterical.

Bethany fights desperately to come fully awake, clear her own head and grasp why her mother is so mad and shouting at her. Through the chaos Bethany comprehends a word here and there... "died" ... "Mrs. Blanchard" ... "devastated" ... "WHY?"

Ryan is now also fully awake and sits in wide-eyed horror as he watches his mother unravel on his sister. He begins to cry thinking he's next!

Bethany utters words of explanation but are inaudible to Rachel in her hysteria. Growing concerned that she may actually strike Bethany in her frenzy, she orders her to her room, then turns toward Ryan and issues the same command. Rachel has never struck any of her children, other than a light tap on the butt to drive her message home. Both children retreat without haste, sobbing all the way up the carpeted stairs to the sanctity of their room.

Bethany slams the bedroom door shut, then grabs Ryan by the arm and together they crouch at the foot of Bethany's bed in fear of what may happen next; for they've never seen their mother so upset and can't begin to comprehend what punishment may follow.

Bethany begins to hum...Ryan recognizes the tune and joins in chorus... "Row, row, row your boat, gently down the stream..." This has become Bethany's means of turning off the scary stuff and so continues its melody until....

Twenty minutes have past. Bethany and Ryan now sit in silence, unmoved from the same spot they sought in their retreat. An occasional sniff is the only sound that emits from their tiny forms.

They come to full alert, hearing muffled voices from the floor below. "Daddy!" "Daddy's home!" They realize that Mommy and Daddy are most likely talking about what happened which renews their fear about the imminent punishment to come.

Within minutes, the door to their inner sanctum slowly opens wide and there before them stands their father, Larry with a red-eyed mother, Rachel, close behind. Bethany and Ryan are speechless as their father enters the room and then speaks in a slow, surprisingly low tone. He begins, "Bethany, Mommy told me what happened today. What I want to know is why you said those things to Mrs. Blanchard?" Not sure she should answer, Bethany remains unresponsive. Her father pleads again, only this time with a more insistent tone. "Bethany! I demand you tell me why you did such a thing."

Realizing that there's no other way around it, Bethany starts to explain... "Daddy, I'm sorry..." then bursts into tears all over again. Feeling softened by his daughter's obvious state, Larry stoops down before his trembling children, gently wiping away Bethany's tears while stroking Ryan's curly hair in parental reassurance. Larry is cognizant of how close Bethany and Ryan are and knows that both his children are in need comforting now, especially if he's to get to the bottom of what's happened.

The conversation resumes: "I know you're sorry, Bethany but what I want to understand is why you said what you did to

Mrs. Blanchard and how you knew Mr. Blanchard was going to heaven?"

Bethany leaps up then wraps both of her tiny arms about her father's neck ever so tightly, almost choking him and whispers, "I saw it. I saw it in my dream, Daddy..." Larry whispers back, "What did you see?" Bethany continues, "The church...Mrs. Blanchard and the others crying...then there was the box." "What box?" her father pleads. "The pretty wooden box with the white sheet over it covered in flowers..." she trails off.

It is clear to Larry that what his daughter is describing is Mr. Blanchard's funeral. Without missing a beat, Larry reaches for Ryan to join in their embrace, which he does without hesitation. Rachel wipes the silent tears that continue to fall from her own face as she watches her husband encircle their children in the safety and consolation of his loving arms.

Larry gently pulls back from their embrace and softly instructs the children to go with their mother to wash their faces and get ready for dinner but not without a firm message of warning to Bethany. "Bethany," he pauses, carefully measuring the words he will utter next. "Bethany, you have...this...uh um...ability to know certain things, see things, that are about to happen to other people...but just because you can see these things doesn't mean you should tell people what you see...", Larry fumbles for a better explanation.

"People will think you're not normal...that you have...um... something they don't and because they can't do what you can... gosh...how do I say this? They will be afraid of you and call you bad names. You don't want that now, do you?"

Bethany nods her head in agreement but is still unsure of what he wants her to do. He's about to make it all much clearer. "I don't want you to do this ever again, Bethany! Do you understand? I forbid you to tell anyone what you see? I mean it...never again!" Bethany looks deep in her father's eyes hoping he'd understand...perhaps he does, more than she knows but for the time being she needs to follow his orders completely. "Okay, Daddy...I won't...I promise..."

With that, Larry tenderly kisses both his children on their foreheads and tells them to wash up for dinner...there will be no more talk about this, not even to Charlie. Enough said.

THE KEEPER

*L*ike I said, I remember everything! When I was three years
old, I contracted viral meningitis and I have to tell you, I
was one sick kid. Life was a bit of a blur for me during that time,
so when I began having visits from odd looking children with
big black eyes and oversized heads in a place I referred to as the
"play house", it was hard for me to discern what was real and
what was a dream or, more likely, hallucinations from my fever,
which was my mother's opinion.

I clearly remember hearing a low, vibrational humming sound
before each visit. Very shortly after the sound began, I actually
saw swirls of energy that formed before me. At first, they were
colorless; then as they drew ever closer, they burst into deep
colors of crimson, cobalt blue, neon green, vibrant yellow and
deep purple. I was so entranced by this whirling spectacle that I
hadn't noticed how I had become a part of it, as I levitated and
floated silently into its core.

Never, EVER was I afraid, nor did I scramble to retreat. I
simply allowed it to unfold, curious to see where I was being
led; not concerned in the least about whether or not I was in any
danger. Strange…I know.

As I floated through this maze of twisting colors, I began
moving faster and faster, and it was only then that I became
fearful of how I would exit. Would I come to a crashing halt or
what other method would bring this uncontrollable speed to end?

The faster I traveled, the louder the humming was, to the point
that I covered my ears with my hands and slammed my eyes shut
tightly hoping this would all just stop. And then it happened…
all was quiet, no more sound, eerily silent.

I knew I wasn't floating anymore and yet I felt deliciously light. One by one, I slowly opened each eye and to my surprise and delight, there before me was a room filled with toys of every kind. The walls were ablaze with colorful images of blue skies dotted with white fluffy clouds, renderings of every animal there ever was, images of oceans, rivers and amazing waterfalls, fields of flowers and lush green forests.

I thought I was alone, but then a ghostly figure slowly emerged and began to come into focus. It was tall and very thin. Its head was huge! It had dead black, almond shaped, slanted eyes; its lips were so narrow, I wasn't sure there were any there at all, nor did I see any semblance of ears. I remember thinking, what odd arms, so long and skinny, as they hung unmoving by its side.

Just when I was about to cry out, I heard a voice, not speaking aloud but in my head, that said... "Don't be afraid...no one will hurt you here..." As I attempted to grasp the words, for they certainly didn't match my feelings of safety, the voice continued... "You have been chosen to be part of this...you are a special child...fear not for you are not alone...others are here with you and for you."

I was about to speak aloud, "Who are you?" but as the words were forming in my head, the voice answered my thought... "I am The Keeper...Welcome Bethany!"

(Flashback)

As The Keeper reaches down for young Bethany's hand, she is understandably reluctant to reach back. When she does, she giggles nervously as the skin of the being's hand feels a little like a beach ball to her, somewhat rubbery, slippery and cool to the touch. Definitely not like holding Mommy's or Daddy's hand.

With her hand now engulfed in that of The Keeper's, Bethany tilts her head to the side examining the form more intensely then asks out loud... "Hey! Where's the rest of your fingers?" The Keeper continues its forward momentum but responds as before, (telepathically), *These ARE my only fingers.* Bethany continues her asking... "How come you don't have any ears? And where's your nose? ... and..." The Keeper gives Bethany's hand a gentle tug and points her towards one of many round, brightly colored, tables with four small chairs to match, perfectly sized for children... and others ... who may visit this strange playroom full of toys.

The Keeper pulls a bright blue chair back from one of the tables and indicates for Bethany to sit down, which she does objectionably, folding her arms in across her chest in defiance and offers indignantly ... "You didn't answer my questions...", then lets out a huge sigh in righteous impatience. The Keeper raises one arm in gesture for Bethany to look in another direction, which she does without hesitation, more curious than obedient.

As Bethany looks about the room in wonderment of what will happen next, she notices several other large beings that look similar to The Keeper, each vigilantly standing by unoccupied tables, all in silent expectation.

To Bethany's surprise, a large group of children of all ages burst into the room through a set of double metal doors, cheerfully chattering, some furiously racing to the colorful tables about the room to lay claim on the vacant seats that await. Two other children approach the table where Bethany is seated with little to no acknowledgment of her presence. Wondering if any of this is real, Bethany silently sits as an observer and wonders... Am I dreaming all this?...

The Keeper respond, *No Bethany...this is no dream...*

Once settled, the children's chatter diminishes as they appear to be waiting...but for what? Or should the query more accurately be...for whom?

The Keeper is aware of Bethany's confusion and in anticipation of her next question relays a non-verbal, *Here they come... this is why you are here!*

Bethany slowly turns her head in the same direction the other children's attention has been drawn to and there before her enters a parade of ...*what are they? Are they kids like me? They don't look like me?*

Slowly and without fanfare, the strange looking beings file into the room, seemingly taking preassigned seating at these colorful tables where the human children patiently wait. Like miniature versions of The Keeper, these odd forms, with enlarged heads and big eyes, greet their human counterparts with little to no emotion.

Bethany's eyes closely follow three specific beings whose destination is clearly the table where she and the other human children are seated. But these forms are different from the rest for they appear more...human. One has a tuft of red hair atop its odd shaped head, while another seems to have teeth that it robotically displays in a most peculiar way. Bethany can't help but liken this forced grin to those moments when her parents are about to take a picture of she and Ryan and instruct, "Smile! Say cheese!" That's the constant look this being has on its face. Kinda scary, Bethany thinks.

But the being that sits next to Bethany appears more human than all the others. This being has more hair and has ears! They are somewhat smaller in size and look a bit misshapen, however, Bethany's perception of what is odd is quickly changing by the minute.

But what she finds to be most captivating is the color of this being's eyes, for they are the brightest, crystal blue hue she has ever seen!

All logic and basic reason aside, Bethany likes this being and feels a smile beginning to form about her mouth, which the being emulates back to her.

The Keeper begins to speak, his thin lips never moving, but his words are clearly heard:

Welcome to all! We are pleased to have you join us again. Some of you are new to our program so we will explain why you are here and what you are to do while you are in our presence.

Bethany, not yet fully engaged into what is being said, is beyond curious on HOW she's able to hear these words that are apparently coming from The Keeper, yet his mouth isn't moving one bit! Her eyes quickly scan the room for an alternate source, then darts her glance back towards The Keeper and ponders... How is he doing that?

The Keeper continues:

You have been chosen by those of our planet and yours to be part of an experiment...one that will be of great importance to all. We will do our best to speak words you will understand and... most prominently... wish to convey that you are safe ... no one will harm you here.

At this point, The Keeper stops his telepathic transmission and looks down directly at Bethany, who returns the gaze in wide-eyed total confusion. Realizing that Bethany's language skills, while exceptional given her young age, are still a bit rudimentary for this conversation, in particular to comprehending the high level of knowledge The Keeper is about to relay.

Bending down, he softly places both hands about Bethany's head for but a moment. Bethany responds by closing her eyes and emits a slow and easy sigh. Knowing that what was needed to understand him fully has been accomplished, The Keeper resumes:

We are beings from an alternate galaxy and dimension. We are often referred to as Extraterrestrials (E.T.s), by your planet's inhabitants, however, we prefer the term Star Beings. We have come a great distance to observe and learn your ways. Your planet has much to offer and so it is that we wish to help you nourish and keep it sustainable.

In your world and in your language, we are perceived, rightfully so, as an advanced civilization possessing higher technologies that Earth's inhabitants know nothing of, nor do they partake. For the younger humans, I would explain it this way…we know how to do astonishing things that might appear as magic but I assure you, it is not. We have learned how to manipulate energy and project thought to one another without the use of vocal language. We understand the natural order of our environments to the degree of working in cooperation with it, rather than with great resistance. I hope that helps…(pause)…your level of communication is a bit difficult for us, as we haven't used actual language for what in Earth terms would be unexplainable. But I will continue…

We are also highly advanced technicians; in your world you would refer to us as scientists, physicists and biologist who study all manner of living things. We know of that which is seen, and cognizant of that which is unseen.

Since we are a more significantly evolved species, our message will be transmitted at the level you are at in your humanness and considered brain capacity. Language between diverse species is quite complex. As noted on Earth, your inhabitants speak many languages, so it becomes necessary to either learn that language or remain disconnected in your differences.

Our advanced evolution has rendered voice transmission unnecessary in our world and so, we are challenged in our communication with humans...(pause)... but the essence of what is being relayed to you will be known at the deepest core of your being.

There is not one of your species who cannot absorb our intention or mission as long as your heart is pure and your soul yearns for the highest good for all.

As we progress through this experiment, alterations may be necessary in our forms of transportation and communication. This is a big part of the program...to find a way of communication and travel between our dimensions and ways of being that will bring a greater understanding to those of separation. For we are all one, even in our divide.

We have chosen to work with the youngers rather than the elders who have been contaminated by those who wish to maintain dominance and control of your planet. The youngers up to this point, remain accepting and have not yet separated from that which they truly are and have remembering of their non-human abilities that will, in time, if not utilized, become an enigma and will dissipate its usefulness.

For now, we will assist in the enhancement of those...um... unique abilities and will utilize them to teleport you to this place of teaching those considered our youngers, with the intention of knowing the ways of this planet so that we may walk among earthlings undetected. For if we were to reveal ourselves fully, much disorder would ensue and the program would cease.

You will remember these visits and interactions...only know that those with whom you will share this information, if not part of the program themselves, will not understand and view your statements as dysfunctional and perhaps even harmful. Discern that none of that is true.

Know that what you are a part of is for the highest good of all. You are the future of your planet and will usher Earth's inhabitants into the greater galaxies with expanded knowledge *and purpose. Go now...work with the youngers that sit before you...embrace the mission for which YOU have been chosen!*

SCHOOL DAYS, SCHOOL DAYS, BREAK THEM GOLDEN RULES DAYS!

When it came time for me to enroll into kindergarten, my parents were apprehensive, to say the least, but they thought that my interaction with "normal" kids may be just the thing to rid me of what became termed as my "fantasy world."

Bizarre as it may seem, a lesser known fact that would be revealed later on, was that more than one family member had the same...um, shall we say...talents? Oh, I knew Ryan 'got me', for he would display his own abilities, every now and then, by way of our telepathic conversations. More often than not, he'd burst in, grab onto my arm, pulling as hard as he could, indicating that I was to follow him; usually to a more private spot where he would relay an awkward message; (remember, he was still a year and a half younger than me, so his language skills were still a work in progress – all the more reason our telepathic communications kicked into high gear).

Here's a good example: One morning, after Charlie had left for school, Ryan came flying into our communal bedroom in a panic. As I attempted to tune into Ryan to fathom what all the fuss was about, Ryan "showed me", via telepathic image that Charlie was about to be ambushed by one of his classmates, who obviously held some grudge about Charlie wining the attention of a young lady that he had hoped to have all to himself. I guess middle school flirtations were often held in earnest as a prerequisite for the battle of the fittest. So, for all intents and purposes, even at his pre-teenagerhood (is that a word?) the dawning of the *macho-male hunter/gatherer role was evident, being cultivated, and undeniably alive and well in brother Charles.*

From what Ryan relayed to me in our special communication was that Charlie held his own but, nonetheless, was about to arrive home with a very big black and blue eye that would be the talk of the school for months to come.

About the time Charlie was due home from school, Ryan and I hot footed ourselves downstairs to the kitchen where we knew he would soon enter, plunk down his backpack onto the kitchen counter, then head straight for the refrigerator to grab a soda, which was his daily routine. Mom was usually positioned somewhere close by around this time of day, whether in the adjacent laundry room finishing up the daily washing or involved in an early dinner preparation. As fate would have it, Mom was planted at the kitchen table peeling potatoes when the hour of truth approached. Just his luck!

"What are you two troublemakers up to?", my Mom astutely asked, not yet clued into the real reason behind our hasty entrance into the kitchen, looking like two anticipatory cats waiting to pounce on an unsuspecting mouse. Enter Charles...

To his credit, Charlie did his best to act normal, albeit always keeping the left side of his face just out of Mom's view - the side that held the shiner. And it worked for all of two minutes until Ryan let out a, "Wow! Does that hurt a lot?", to which our Mom spun around to inquire... "Does what hurt a lot?"

Before Charlie could reach Ryan to tell him to shut up, Mom spied the injury and with a huge gasp decried, "Charles William Wilcox! Have you been fighting?"

What saved Ryan from getting the wrath of Charlie's 'I'm gonna kill you' look, was that he now had to jump into defensive mode and explain to Mom, and fast, how he'd been jumped by this kid who always had it in for him, blah, blah, blah...

Mom instantly went into the "Oh, you poor kid" mode, which was Ryan's and my cue to high tail it out of the kitchen to the refuse of the backyard and our swing set. For we knew that Mom and Charlie's conversation would carry on for a while longer... which it did.

As Ryan and I pretended to busy ourselves on the swing set, we were able to overhear an occasional earful with snippets from Mom's voice ... "You know fighting isn't right..." and then we'd hear Charlie pleading ... "but you don't understand..."

Ryan and I looked over at one another in mid swing and began to giggle as little children do, with the full knowledge that we could never tell anyone our little secret; how we already knew that Charlie had been sucker punched by this kid at school and sported the colorful swollen eye in testimony. So, every once in a while, our precognitive skills brought us a bit of entertainment, even if at Charlie's expense.

Ryan and I were always getting into mischief in one form or another. A few weeks before my sixth birthday, Mom and Dad announced that it was time for me to start kindergarten, which I viewed as an attempt to break up Ryan's and my dynamic duo. But I took it in stride and actually was excited at the prospect. So, all in all, everything seemed normal...until...

(Flashback)

Rachel is thrilled, albeit a bit apprehensive when Bethany's first day of kindergarten finally arrives. She nervously goes about her morning routine of feeding her family and making lunch for Charlie and packing a healthy mid-morning snack for Bethany. Larry is seated at the head of the kitchen table, perusing work papers that he inches out of his briefcase in preparation of his early morning meeting with clients, all the while sipping his second cup of coffee, somewhat oblivious to the children's routine.

Ryan slumps in his seat, pushing his food around the plate, sulking that he can't go to school with Bethany and mopes about... now who will I play with? Larry tries to console Ryan by stating how Bethany will be home right around lunch time, so he'll only have the morning to himself. No such luck. All Ryan knows is that Bethany is leaving him behind...just like when she visits the play house and he is having none of it.

Bethany, on the other hand, is off the charts excited and barely eats her breakfast and ignores her mother's pleas to finish her French toast before jetting off up the stairs to her bedroom closet to put on her new school attire. Rachel allows Bethany to pick out her own outfit for her first day, just so long as she doesn't look ridiculous, throwing on patterns or colors that don't match at all.

Bethany, who normally votes for denim jeans over anything else, chooses a sweet blue, white and soft green plaid dress with a lace collar that has a matching sash, which her mother expertly ties around the back into the perfect bow.

Next, she carefully selects a pair of light blue socks that compliment her dress perfectly, then reaches for her brand new, shiny black shoes. When Rachel offers to assist in the buckling process, a firm and determined Bethany insists - "I can do it...I can DO it!" "Okay! Okay, Missy. Just trying to help and speed things along so you're not late on your first day", Rachel shoots back with a chuckle.

Rachel wants to add a lovely blue hair ribbon to complete the ensemble but Bethany waves her hand in the air indicating – that's a negative. She wants her hair to hang without restriction, so no hair bows today. Done!

Ryan follows the chaos in silence, his head hangs low in acceptance of being the only one at home with Mom. Such is the life of the baby of the family. It doesn't matter that everyone told him that before he knows it, he'll be going off to school. It just isn't happening today and that is that.

With Bethany adorned in her new school clothes and Ryan in tow, he emits an occasional sniffle for the quintessential dramatic effect, Rachel loads her young family into their car seats, double checking to ensure everyone is secure and ready to go.

Bethany reaches across at her younger sibling and gives him a smile, then reassures him that she'll be back home in no time and promises that they will have more than enough time to play together. Ryan manages to return a meager acknowledging smile back at his big sister. Rachel witnesses this tender moment between her two children when she gives a quick glance in her rearview mirror and radiates a smile of her own. Proud Mama, indeed!

When they arrive at the elementary school, both children stare in wide-eyed amazement. Whatever trepidation Bethany is experiencing, she's keeping it close to her vest. "Come on, kids!", Rachel says cheerfully, as she unbuckles each car seat and places her offspring gently onto the parking lot pavement. Rachael does her best to keep her own emotions in check for fear of setting off a deluge of tears from the rest of the clan.

Once inside, Rachel and the children are greeted by a sea of children's faces of varying ages, in a noisy, echoing hallway. With her children flanked on either side, Rachel holds their hands fast, partially in reassurance, most likely unwittingly from her own apprehension.

The scene is chaotic, but before true panic can set in, Bethany is met by a friendly and somewhat familiar face...that of her kindergarten teacher, Ms. Holloway, whom she met when Rachel brought her here for enrollment some weeks before.

"You're a breath of fresh air!", Rachel whispers to Ms. Holloway who chuckles softly indicating she understands what she means.

"Good morning, Bethany. I'm so happy to see you. And who is this handsome young man with you?" Bethany looks around wondering what young man she is referring to, then gets a light tug from her mother's hand and says, "Ms. Holloway wants you to introduce your brother to her", Rachel instructs Bethany.

"Oh, um… this is my brother, Ryan. He's not old enough yet to go to school.", Bethany responds. Ryan quickly takes his cue to reiterate how upset he is that he can't join his big sister, to which Ms. Holloway crouches down close to him and gives him a little wink and says, "Well, Mr. Ryan, now you have something very special to look forward to soon, don't you?", she quips with a questioning look at mother Rachel.

"It will be more like the following year, as Ryan's birthday falls just short of next year's registration", Rachel states with a bit of hesitation, in hopes that doesn't upset Ryan further. Both women are keenly aware of children's sense of time and how distant and seemingly forever things appear to them if it's not immediate.

"Okay, Bethany, if you're ready, this would be a good time to say goodbye to Mom and Ryan and we'll see them again very soon when they pick you up in a few hours." Bethany glances briefly at her brother then more longingly at her mother before responding, somewhat timidly, "Ready."

Without hesitation, Ms. Holloway gently reaches for Bethany's hand in an effort to not prolong the farewells. Bethany slowly retreats her grip on her mother's hand and lets Ms. Holloway take the lead and off they go to her classroom to meet with the other children.

In all honestly, Bethany isn't exactly sure what to expect. Since she'd already been interacting with other children and hybrids in the play house, she can't help but wonder if this will be the same type of environment; but determines it probably won't be exactly the same...unless the hybrids are here too!

The classroom is small in comparison to the play house and in lieu of the colorful tables and chairs, instead Bethany finds actual individual seats attached to a small desktop. Each desk has the children's names spelled out in bright, bold lettering. It is the teacher's expectation that each child can at least recognize their own name and take their designated seats. Didn't always work out that way, however.

While Ms. Holloway escorts others to their proper seat, Bethany finds hers with no trouble. Taking her place, she begins to look about the room and is somewhat pleased to see colorful images of animals, flowers and trees, similar to what she experienced in the "play house" setting.

When all are seated, Ms. Holloway again introduces herself to the class and welcomes one and all to their new school. "Now that I've introduced myself to you, I think it would be fun to have each one of you come up here by me, so you can introduce yourselves to the rest of the class." There is a low gasp from some of the children who are perhaps a bit shy. "Who would like to go first...raise your hand..."

"I will!" shouts a boy who is seated in the middle of the room. The name on his desk read J-A-C-K, last names were not indicated on these name plates.

"Okay, then Jack, come on up here by me and let's get to know you better." Jack raced up to the front of the class, almost tripping in his haste. The class lets out a giggle as Ms. Holloway instructs him to begin. "Jack, tell us your name, if you have any brothers or sisters and what is special or interesting about you that you'd like us to know - like what things do you like to do for fun."

As Jack starts his narration, Bethany immediately begins to squirm in her seat in anticipation of her turn. Never considered shy in any way, all of a sudden Bethany finds her heart pounding fast and hard in her chest, making it almost impossible to pay attention to what Jack is sharing with his new classmates.

Faster and faster her heart races and then the room begins to spin, to the point where she knows she needs to somehow settle herself down. Remembering the little trick she had discovered when the barrage of unexplainable visions was thrust upon her, she found that singing "Row, Row, Row Your Boat Gently Down the Stream", always put things right again.

Waiting for her turn to speak before the class certainly qualifies as one of those unnerving moments and so she covers her mouth and softly begins humming to herself, barely audible to those around her... *Row, row, row your boat...gently down the stream...merrily, merrily, merrily, merrily...*

"Bethany, is everything alright?" Ms. Holloway's voice breaks in, disrupting her melodic refrain. Bethany struggles to bring herself back into the room to answer her teacher's question. Inside she's screaming, *No! No! No! Don't make me stop singing!* then anxiously blurts... "Yes! Yes, Ms. Holloway, I'm okay."

"Good! Would you like to come up to say hello to the class so we can all get to know you better?" This is the last thing Bethany wants to do but she's making every effort to fit in and be like the other children...but can she?

Looking like the proverbial deer in the headlights, Bethany now stands before her peers, her shallow breaths barely allows the air to pass over her vocals chords to make any sound that would be intelligible. Ms. Holloway urges her on... "Class, this is Bethany...go on honey..."

"M-m-y n-name is Be-Bethany"... she stutters, then glancing over to her teacher who gestures with her hands to continue... "I-I..um..er...er...I have two brothers...Charlie, who is...older

than me...and...um...Ry-Ryan who is my baby brother."
Bethany hears Ms. Holloway ask her to go on and tell the class
what's special about her...what she likes to do. Oh gosh...here
I go...

Bethany begins her tale of the "play house and how she knows
things before they happen, then pauses. Her teacher seems
intrigued yet guarded as she urges her to continue and to share
with the class an example of her knowing things.

Bethany's head begins to roar as the obligatory flow of
information, wanted or unwanted, streams from her pouted lips.
Hesitantly, she points to one child after the other and shares
visions and thoughts that come through as if watching a movie.

Unable to control the flow of information, nor the speed in
which the premonitions are being presented in her head, Bethany
starts walking up and down the desk laden isles; confidently
delivering the messages to each classmate: "You're not going on
the trip to Disney Land because your Uncle Jim is going to die"
... then to another child; "You're going to have to move because
your daddy isn't coming back...he's left you and your mom...";
and then, to yet another... "Your neighbor has a bad lump in his
head and he's not going to be around anymore..."

"Bethany! Stop!" Ms. Holloway shouts, unable to control her
own shock as this beautiful, innocent looking five-year old child
speaks such unfathomable words to her unsuspecting classmates.

The classroom is now filled with uncontrollable sobbing from
the children Bethany has graced with her wisdom. Shaking herself
free from her shock of what has just taken place, Ms. Holloway
reaches aggressively for Bethany's arm and hastily escorts her
out of the classroom, leaving behind an unruly and disruptive
group of kindergarteners, yelling and sobbing in chorus.

Bethany begins to cry, not so much that her teacher's grip
is causing her pain, but because she realizes that she's done it
again...gone too far with her "knowings" and becomes fearful

of the unknown punishment that is sure to follow. But more frightening to Bethany is the thought of facing her parents... *Please don't tell my Mommy and Daddy about this!!!*

LIZ

*S*o, there I was - this five-year old kid who was beginning to freak everyone out on my first day of kindergarten, no less. Knowing what was going to happen before it actually did wasn't enough for me – no! I had to go ahead and share my play house interactions with an alien hybrid to anyone who'd listen. Yeah, that definitely was the final straw for my parents; my mother, in particular.

Oh, she tried desperately to understand, even began playing along with my stories, you know, the way a parent would when confronted with a child who had an imaginary playmate...only mine was real!

In the beginning, I didn't know what was happening and so on my return teleportation from the play house, I don't mind telling you that I was one scared little girl. Now couple that with my precognitive visions and clairaudient voices... well you can only imagine.

So, what do I do? Like most kids who have to deal with unusual or, in my case, unique travel experiences, I created my own coping mechanism that seemed to work for me just fine. In an effort to turn "off" the information/feelings that I am getting, I simply utilized my old standby, "Row, Row, Row, Your Boat, Gently Down the Stream" seemed to do the trick. By the time I finish the last line, "life is but a dream", the images and feelings are gone...at least for a while. How long? It varies. If it's something really strong, it can immediately come back at me. But for the most part I can give myself several hours of peace before I'm bombarded once again. I've accepted this "gift" and *for the most part I'm okay with it. Like I said...for the most part.*

Ryan was cool with it all and asked me all kinds of questions and would get really upset when he found out he couldn't go to the play house with me. Ryan actually observed my transportation on more than one occasion and when he relayed that to my mother, she felt that whatever my issue was, was now influencing and affecting him and she couldn't allow that. One overly imaginative child was enough... but not two!

Consequently, that's when my parents sought out a child psychologist, but not just any psychologist; they actually were fortunate enough to locate a woman who specialized in "children like me", who dealt with precognitive abilities and claims of close encounters with alien beings. That was me, alright. In spades!

Her name was Elizabeth Tanner Wolf...she liked me to call her Liz. Little did I know at the time how important Liz would be in helping my parents accept what I knew to be my reality. But more importantly, for me to openly embrace the apparent role I was playing with the hybrids. A uniquely, specific role for which I was chosen. But there was more...

(Flashback)

Bethany sits fidgeting in the chair, feet swinging back and forth as they barely reach the carpet of the waiting room floor of the child psychologist's office. Loudly smacking the wad of bubble gum that takes up the majority of her tiny mouth, she manages to ask her mother, "Will it be much longer?" Looking down lovingly from the seat next to Bethany, her mother, Rachel, gently pats the back of her daughter's hand as she impatiently drums her fingers in nervous, annoying rhythm and answers, "Soon, baby...soon."

Rachel is still uncomfortable with having to take her beloved daughter to a child psychologist but knows that she has no other choice, for Bethany's visions and predictions are ever increasing. The most disturbing element for Rachel is Bethany's insistence that she goes to a special "play house" via some mode of teleportation to interact with beings from another world! That's all Rachel and Larry had to hear to solidify their decision to get their daughter help...and fast!

Within moments, the inner office door of child psychologist Elizabeth Tanner Wolf swings wide open as eight-year-old Michael bounds out of his session, his Attention Deficit Disorder diagnosis evident to all that bear witness.

"See you next week, Michael", Liz calls as he races down the hallway, leaving his bewildered father behind, shaking his head and rolling his eyes as he prepares to sprint after his son who, most likely, has already reached the elevator by now.

"Hi Liz!" shouts an excited Bethany. "Well, hello there, Ms. Bethany! And how are you today?" Liz responds with a warm and engaging smile. Liz knows she's not supposed to have favorites but she allows herself to openly show her pleasure at seeing Bethany at each and every visit. Bethany has been coming to these sessions for over a month now and is openly excited to have someone listen and believe what she is about to share.

"Ready?", asks Liz.

"Ready!", answers Bethany.

"Let's go! See you in a little bit, Mom.", Liz reassures Rachel.

Liz takes Bethany's small hand in hers and leads her into the private office. Once inside, Bethany immediately hops onto a soft, overstuffed chair that's designed especially low to the ground for smaller patients.

Bethany feels very comfortable in this environment for the office is well appointed with soothing colors of sea foam green and earth tone beige. The walls are featured with special images of clear blue skies dotted with puffy white clouds, fields of colorful flowers that seem to go on forever, and a star filled night sky that seems to beckon the observer far and away into the galaxies beyond.

Bethany states to Liz how much she likes the images on her walls, which remind her of the colorful images on the walls of the play house where she meets with alien hybrids

Liz also thought it would be fun, as well as practical, to have all manner of drawing and coloring materials with wads of blank paper for those moments of inspiration, when words just aren't enough to describe...

When the older kids are in session with Liz, she utilizes soft, relaxing music or recorded whale and ocean sounds on her CD player. It has been her experience that the mature kids are inclined to open up and focus more fully with these particular background sounds.

But not so with the little ones. Unfortunately, it has the total opposite effect on the younger set. They become too aware of and focused on the music and begin to dance or interpret the animal sounds by performing a kind of charades ... "Look at me...I'm a whale!"

Because sessions with the children don't always remain on track, Liz agrees with the method of tape recording them, a trick she learned from her days with Dr. Ortega, the amazing child psychologist that both Liz and her husband, Stephan saw as young children; as they, too, experienced other worldly encounters. This way she can re-listen, evaluate and then later transcribe their conversations.

Liz normally turns on the recorder undetected by most of the children who, most assuredly, would ask a million questions about it and begin performing instead of focusing on today's visit. But with Bethany, Liz always asks... "Ready to record, Ms. Bethany?", to which Bethany responds with a smile... "Sure."

Liz begins:	*Okay, sweetie, so tell me...what's been happening lately? Gone on any trips with your friends?*
Bethany:	*Oh sure. Just last night I went to the play house with the others and we had lots of fun!*
Liz:	*Tell me about the play house, again?*
Bethany:	*Well, it's where we go to show the others how to play nicely with the toys. They're so funny... sometimes they hold them wrong...upside down like this.* (She demonstrates with her hands to indicate flipping something over – upside down.)
Liz:	*Oh, that is funny. Tell me, Bethany, have they learned to talk to you with words, yet?*
Bethany:	*Uh, uh - not yet. But I hear them anyway...in my head. The Keeper says it saves having to use the words. When they do make sounds, they sound funny and I laugh.* (Bethany giggles.)
Liz:	*Do they laugh, too?*
Bethany:	*No, but I know they like what we're doing.*

All the while this dialog is going on, Bethany is roaming around the room, picking up books and examining stuffed animals that lay about. As long as she continues to remain focused on the questions, Liz allows her to do her thing.

Liz asks Bethany to elaborate more on The Keeper and if she would like to draw a picture him/her (as even Bethany isn't sure if The Keeper is a boy or a girl) and of her friends and what it looks like at the play house.

"No, not right now. Besides, I already did that before... remember?" Bethany reminds Liz. "I told you...The Keeper is tall, very tall...is skinny and doesn't have a mouth. We talk to one another in our heads...did you forget?"

Liz responds, "Of course, now I remember, thanks for reminding me."

Bethany goes on to remind Liz that she's drawn enough pictures of the play house and doesn't feel like doing it again. "I already did that a million times...(sighs) don't you remember?", she states with a hint of exasperation in her voice.

"Yes, I certainly do and you did such a great job." Liz assures. "I just wondered if this time, it looked any different to you or, if there was anything or anyone new to the play house."

Bethany suddenly stops her roaming about and stares skyward, as if trying to remember something and says, "We-e-l-l, yes, actually...there were some new playmates that I didn't know. They were kinda bigger...like this much." (Again, Bethany demonstrates with her hands held high above her head.)

Liz: *Did you play with any of them?*

Bethany: *Not really, they just sorta watched.*

Bethany resumes her stroll about the office seemingly unaffected by the barrage of questions. Liz decides this new revelation deserves more focus from Bethany, so she gently urges her to pick up whatever drawing implement she chooses and asks her to draw, as best she can, what the new playmates look like.

As Bethany picks up a box of crayons and spills its contents onto the carpet, Liz grabs a piece of blank paper from the supply shelf and plops herself down next to her, sitting Indian style, keeping quiet while Bethany intensely sketches her encounter with her new friends.

It is Bethany who finally breaks the silence by commenting on how she doesn't feel very good about one of the larger playmates, who seems "kinda mean."

Liz finds an appropriate moment to resume their conversation:

Liz: *Why do you say that? Don't you like him?*

Bethany: *I dunno...he just makes me feel...um..er...like he looks mad or something. I stop playing with the others when he's around and he gets mad, I think.*

Liz: *Why do you stop playing?*

Bethany: *Well, first of all, I got knocked down...* (Liz waits). *He comes in and just looks at me...* (She trails off engrossed in her sketching.)

Liz: *Who knocked you down, sweetie?*

Bethany: *One of the others, one of my play friends.*

Liz: *Why do you suppose he did that?*

Bethany: *It's a she...and she got mad because I was playing with a toy she wanted.*

Liz: *Oh.* (Liz can't help but draw the conclusion that "kids will be kids" no matter the species.) *How did she knock you down?*

Bethany: (Before Liz can give Bethany any options of method how this was done, she blurts out), *With her mind! She pushed me down with her mind! They don't like to touch very much so they do it in their heads, just like how we talk...in our heads.*

Liz concludes telepathy and kinetics are at work here.

Liz: *Bethany, what did you do when you got knocked down like that?*

Bethany: *Oh, I cried and when I got up. I went over to her and yelled in her face with my outside voice to STOP IT!* (She demonstrates with a yell.)

Liz:	(Stifling a snicker) *What did she do then?*
Bethany:	*She ran over to one of the big friends who was watching and hid behind her. Maybe the big one is her mommy?*
Liz:	*Perhaps. So, tell me...what happened next?*

Just then Bethany hollers "FINISHED!" and holds up her drawing. "Wow! That's very good, Bethany." Liz praises, "Good job! Let's see...hm-m-m...tell me about this." "I just did." Bethany states with obvious impatience. Then indignantly elaborates anyway: "Here I am playing with my friends and here's the big ones watching."

Liz, no stranger to encounters with other beings, recognizes the larger ones as the "Grays" that she, too, interacted with as a small child. She suspects they are the ones responsible for Bethany's abductions, as indicated by her previous drawings of the hybrid children. While more human in appearance, they still had the undeniable big, black, slanted eyes associated with the Zeta Reticuli. Now, it was confirmed.

Liz's focus lands on one of Bethany's drawings of a being with bright, blue eyes and hair and begins to ask about it.

| Liz: | *So, what can you tell me about this one...the friend with the pretty blue eyes...* |
| Bethany: | *Oh, you mean Daphne? I like her...she's nice and doesn't push me.* |

Liz can't help but notice how this friend is more humanoid and less threatening to Bethany. Before Liz can pose the next question, Bethany blurts out... "Are we done, yet?", breaking Liz's concentration on the picture and brings her back into the moment.

"Ah, yep. Actually, we are done!", Liz declares as she spies the clock on her desk. How did she know that? Did she know it or was it just her way of saying she's had enough for today?

Anyway, this is one of the parts she loves the best working with these kids...their total candor and ability to switch gears instantly. But then, she remembers her own experiences and how it became paramount to be able to do just that, or else go mad.

Kids roll with all kinds of stuff, but adults tend to over analyze and dissect... like Liz is doing right now.

Knowing the drill, Bethany puts all the crayons away without being asked to, humming as she continues to chew on the large wad of gum still in her mouth.

All the kids hum now and then but the melody Bethany is humming is not notes of a traditional song. They're more tonal in structure.

Liz: *Do you like to sing Bethany?*

Bethany: *Yep.*

Liz: *What's your favorite song to sing?*

Bethany thinks for a moment then replies:

Bethany: *We-l-l-l, I sing* (she begins - 'Row, Row, Row, Your Boat, Gently Down the Stream'... then stops...) *It's not one of my favorites, but it helps to make it go away..."*

Liz: *Make what go away?*

Bethany: *You know...the bad stuff...the stuff that makes me scared. It helps me make it go away.*

As Liz rises from her seated position on the carpet, she hears Bethany humming yet another song and askes:

Liz: *Hey, that's a nice song you were just humming. I know it's not 'Row, Row, Row Your Boat', so what is it? Did you learn that at school?*

Bethany: *Nope. It's what I hear at the play house with my friends. We all hum it, except they do it in their heads...always in their heads! Gosh, when are they gonna talk like me?*

Liz: *Do they try?*

Bethany: *Sometimes, but* (she's now in full laugh and hard to understand)*...but all that comes out is...ekgt, gloaub, naretty, gleebik...* (inaudible sounds.).

Liz joins Bethany in full laughter as the two embrace and then leads her young charge back to the waiting room and her mother, Rachel.

As Bethany takes her mother's hand in hers, Rachel looks questioningly back over her shoulder at Liz, who reassures her with a wink and a smile then softly says to them both, "See you next week."

AND WHAT IF IN YOUR SLEEP...

***

What if you slept,
And what if in your sleep, you dreamed?
And what if in your dream,
You went to heaven and there you plucked
A strange and beautiful flower?
And what if, when you awoke,
You had the flower in your hand?
Samuel Taylor Coleridge (1771-1834)

(Flashback)

Liz's interest in Bethany goes far beyond that of patient and clinician. Notwithstanding her intense psychic talents, her high level of telepathic communication abilities with the hybrids, not to mention her matter of fact acceptance to all that she has experienced, Bethany has found a way into Liz's heart more than most of her gifted charges.

While Liz chose to keep her own true identity, as well as that of husband Stephan, enigmatic, choosing to specialize in working with "kids like us" meant having compassionate knowledge and understanding of the challenges of living in a limited three-dimensional world; not to mention the ridicule and distrust others displayed unabashedly towards these unique children.

Knowing that the only way Liz can truly find out how Bethany is able to transport between dimensions, she decides to have Bethany participate in a sleep study to monitor and record her brain activity and any other physicality that may prove instrumental to explaining this phenomenon. But how?

Previous methods of obtaining this type of data proved to be cumbersome for the patient, let alone a five-year old child. Liz has been laboring for weeks both in her home office and at the lab, attempting to devise a new and better way to perform this experimental study; one that would be of tremendous clinical value and yet of no physical nor psychological trauma to her precious Bethany. She knows she is close but fears she is running out of options. She cant's help but wonder, Am I losing my clinical objectivity because of my emotional relationship with Bethany? I am too close to all this?

At the insistence of her husband Stephan, Liz takes a break and settles her weary body and brain in the Jacuzzi tub he has lovingly prepared for her, complete with glorious bubbles and scents of Lavender, with an array of dimly lit candles that surrounds the entire enclosure. Soothing sounds of waves crashing upon the shore from the Bose sound system that Stephan has placed atop the vanity provides the finishing touch to this chamber of serenity.

"Okay, okay...I give up!" Liz giggles, flashing one of her, you always know what I need smiles at her beloved husband, as he gingerly backs out of the inner sanctum of the newly created spa, softly closing the door behind him as he exits. Liz slips deeper and deeper into the blissful experience of weightlessness as her body responds to the water's buoyant support and drifts off into peaceful repose.

The next morning, when Stephan awakes to the delectable aroma of coffee brewing, he is greeted by a refreshed and exuberant Liz, who bounds into their bedroom with papers flapping in her hands as she shouts, "Oh my God, Stephan – I've got it! Look!"

With blurred excitement, Stephan struggles to alert comprehensive mode to his wife's prattling description of the drawings that are being whipped past his clouded morning eyes.

Not waiting for her husband's acknowledgement that he's fully awake now to grasp what she's saying, Liz continues; "When I woke up this morning after an amazing good night's sleep...thanks to you, Stephan, it was like I was firing on all cylinders again! I felt compelled to go to my office and began drawing...and this is what came out!" Liz proudly holds up a detailed rendering of what appears to be a round bed floating atop a container that is covered with a clear dome.

She resumes; "Stephan, while I was lying in complete relaxation in the Jacuzzi last night, I began thinking about how young children have the ability to retain the sensation of being in the womb, surrounded by water, that's why they are soothed by rocking, etc. Then I thought, instead of utilizing the electrodes that are normally attached to the head to monitor the brain waves, what if I were to replace them with a domed brain scanner instead... which will create the perfect, non-invasive recording device!"

Stephan, now just as excited as Liz, grabs her in full embrace as he yells, "Brilliant!" Liz chirps in, "Now, it's just a matter of getting a prototype constructed and testing it out before using it on Bethany."

Before Stephan can concur with his wife's declaration, she flies off the bed, bathrobe flying in the breeze as she races to her office to begin making copious notes for her colleagues.

Two weeks later, after countless hours laboring on perfecting this new experimental dome, Liz and her team fuss with the final preparations for Bethany's sleep study, that will begin in just a few short hours. Liz takes one last look around the room, then calmly asks for everyone's attention, nervously clearing her throat to deliver her words of gratitude and praise for a job well done; although under less than desirable conditions, namely her unusual short fuse of late. Even Liz's team is becoming concerned about her lackluster and impatience of late but chalks it up to her need to get this one perfect, for her Bethany.

"I want to thank all of you, most sincerely, for your tireless efforts and long hours away from your own families so that we could stand here today about to make medical research history. I cannot think of any clinicians more talented or individuals more dedicated who could have brought about these amazing results in such a short period of time...again, I thank you." Liz takes in a long, deep breath and squeezes her own two hands behind her back, hoping no one notices how anxious she is as she continues: "Given the nature and sensitivity of this specific subject study with Bethany, I hope you'll understand that I've decided that I'll be the only other person present."

The team's expected moans and gasps were of no surprise and the anticipated evidence of their disapproval is duly noted, but Liz goes on: "Bethany, while a remarkable child, is still just that...a child. I have cultivated and earned her unconditional trust these past several months and cannot jeopardize losing that trust, should she become unsettled with strangers around. So, I will ask that everyone please finish what you were doing and then, you are free to leave."

Liz can feel the heaviness in the room as, one by one, the members of the team silently complete their assigned tasks. She takes one last opportunity to remind them that this study will be recorded and the findings will be reviewed with the entire team upon its completion. Being the professionals that they are, all wish her good luck as they exit the sleep lab.

Liz checks the clock and notes that she has two hours before Bethany and her mother arrive and decides to lock up the lab so that she may retreat to her office for some left-over lasagna she brought from home. She wonders if she'll be able to take a quick power nap in the hope of rejuvenating her understandable fatigue and promises herself to visit with a doctor should she find her energy level does not recuperate once this study is completed.

Liz takes but a few bites of her microwaved dinner and finds it impossible to stay awake. She puts her uneaten meal in the mini-fridge next to her desk then heads over to a small couch by the office door that beckons her to rest. She reaches for the clock that sits adjacent to her temporary bed and thinks it best to set the alarm for one hour from now to ensure she has enough time to fully awake and clear any grogginess that will surely follow.

Liz is amazed at how quickly she relaxes and releases an audible sigh as she drifts off into immediate slumber. Her breathing is deep and steady as her mind slips off into an unconscious state devoid of any time, space, reality.

Before long, she is suddenly jolted back to consciousness as loud music emits from the preset alarm clock radio. The hour passed in the blink of an eye and Liz is somewhat disappointed that she doesn't feel more refreshed. In fact, she finds it quite difficult to walk steadily towards the coffee maker, which she hopes will hold the key to reviving her to a better state of alertness. Unfortunately, the stale tasting coffee offers no assistance and, quite frankly, is making her nauseous, so she wobbles to the small bathroom adjacent to her copy machine and splashes cold water on her sleepy eyes. Liz laughs to herself as she struggles to full consciousness and thinks how she should be the one they're doing the sleep study on, as she hasn't had very much of it lately.

Sitting at her desk, staring at the mish-mash of paperwork that is strewed across the surface in every direction she proclaims, "I really do need to get my act together and get this place more organized." The song from "Annie" rings through her head as she hums the melody "Tomorrow, tomorrow..."

The ringing of her cell phone forces Liz to gather her thoughts as she fumbles to retrieve it, knowing it's buried somewhere beneath the pile of reports on her desk. Finally finding its location she answers, "Hello?" "Hey there, beautiful!", it is her husband Stephan; "Just checking in on you and want to wish you good luck with your study tonight. Everything okay?" Liz forces a cheery "Great! Just doing last minute stuff before Bethany and her Mom arrive, which should be pretty soon, actually. I don't mean to cut you short, sweetie, but I need to get moving and get back to the lab. Don't forget, I'll have my cell phone off for the night, so we'll talk in the morning – okay?"

Before Stephan can answer and say goodbye, Liz lowers her tone and adds, "Stephan, I'm a little nervous about this... is that being unprofessional?" "Are you kidding?" Stephan reassures. "No one has ever done this type of sleep study, especially with a five-year-old...of course you're nervous. But I'll tell you this...I have the utmost faith in you and your devotion to Bethany - so my money is on everything going just perfectly. I love you...call me in the morning. Goodnight."

With that, Liz smiles as she whispers back her words of love to her amazing husband. She takes one last look of herself in the bathroom mirror and gives a wink to the image reflected back and says "Okay, kiddo...it's show time!"

Bethany and her mother, Rachel, arrive right on time and shyly greet Liz, indicating a joint feeling of trepidation about what's going to happen. In an effort to lighten the mood, Liz scoops Bethany up into her arms and twirls her around again and again, bringing about that wonderful giggle of hers, which contagiously makes everyone feel better. Both Bethany and her mother have been briefed many times about the procedure, so it will, hopefully, eliminate some of the anxiety; not so much on Bethany's behalf but for Rachel, who has undoubtedly, got tons of it.

Bethany brought a colorful backpack that Rachel filled with personal artifacts, coloring books and crayons. But her most prized possession that came along for the ride is a long-eared, stuffed bunny she calls Fred, that she holds tightly in her grip.

As Bethany says goodnight to her mother, Liz reminds and reassures her that, "Mommy will be sleeping in a room nearby and will see you first thing in the morning." Bethany asks, "Then I can go home and sleep in my own bed, right? I mean…I..I will be able to see Ry-Ry and Charlie and Daddy tomorrow, right?" Liz is quick to respond in the affirmative with a loving smile and a wink to Bethany, who immediately is distracted by the dome and most assuredly has more questions that need answers. Ahh the incredible, inquisitive mind of this child, Liz muses to herself.

After Rachel exits the lab, leaving Liz and Bethany alone, it is Bethany who breaks the awkward silence to ask, "This won't be scary, will it? I-I don't like the scary stuff…" Liz stoops down to her level and makes direct eye contact with her and says, "If you ever feel that you want to stop, for any reason, just tell me and we will. I promise that you'll be safe and that I'll be right here with you from the time you fall asleep, right up until the moment you wake up in the morning. Okay?" In typical kid fashion, Bethany begins wandering around the room, curiously checking everything out. Question answered…next?

Liz knows that with a child this young and this alert you can't just ask them to lie down and say "let's get this ball rolling", so she unhurriedly assists Bethany in putting on her PJs and then they both head to the rocking chair that Liz has brought in specifically for this purpose of relaxing Bethany before placing her in the special bed chamber.

Bethany and Liz chat easily about many things, and yet nothing along the lines of what Liz expected to encounter, such as; What is that big plastic thing supposed to do? Or, what if I roll off... will I get wet? Or What if I can't fall asleep? ... normal questions a child would ask, and yet Bethany does not.

Liz gets Bethany beyond her clinical understanding of this amazing child's unique abilities and her unearthly experiences and is pleased that she trusts her completely - blatantly evident, in that she settles in with the night's agenda without any fuss.

Liz watches Bethany closely for the cues that the moment of truth has arrived and it's time to move her to the sleep study bed and begin monitoring her brain wave activity. A half-asleep Bethany moans slightly as she is placed in the chamber but easily resumes her slumber.

As several hours pass without incident, Liz finds it challenging to remain awake herself and so drifts off into a light state of rest. Not knowing how long she has been dozing, Liz is brought back to full awareness by the sound of Bethany's voice, that is quite animated as she talks in her sleep.

Bethany is lying on her side with her back facing Liz as her monologue continues. Liz notices the monitors that are recording Bethany's brain activity are indicating that she is not asleep and actually, quite alert.

While Bethany continues her chatter, Liz keeps watching as the data readings intensify and indicate a high level of activity, compelling Liz to leave her chair and move towards the sleep chamber to try to figure out what this all means. If Bethany is awake, is she comforting herself by talking to her stuffed rabbit, Fred?

When Liz finally reaches the chamber, she covers her mouth so as not to startle Bethany who is lying next to an alien hybrid about her size! Unable to speak, Liz continues to watch as Bethany and the hybrid exchange glances and pass the stuffed animal back and forth between them. While Bethany is using audible language, the hybrid is not.

Feeling a bit woozy, Liz grabs for whatever is nearby to steady herself which, ironically, is the outer surface of the domed chamber. With that motion, the hybrid breaks its stare with Bethany and turns its attention to Liz who stands wide eyed leaning against the outside of the dome surface.

Shock turns to melancholy as the hybrid now stares deeply into Liz's eyes. Liz is in complete awe, not just of the hybrid's presence but is hypnotized by the amazing light that emits from its crystal blue eyes that seem to connect to her very soul. No longer freaked out by what she is witnessing, Liz attempts to speak... "B-B-Bethany?" her voice shakes as she asks "Who-who's your friend?"

"She doesn't really have a name but I call her Daphne. I think she likes being called that." Bethany answers matter of factly. "Bethany...c-c-can you tell me how your friend got here?" Liz is almost afraid to hear her answer. "Not sure...but I think when I was playing with her at the play house a little while ago, she asked if she could come back and play at my house, sooo here we are!"

Liz chuckles a nervous laugh and says "Okay, that makes sense. But h-h-how did you both get back here?" Bethany seems a bit exasperated by the question but answers it anyway with "All she has to do is think about it and...poof! Here we are!"

Desperately trying to follow the simple explanation that Bethany provides, Liz's thinks this is anything BUT simple. Her mind is racing trying to figure out if Bethany transported herself to be with her little friend, then transported herself back with her friend in tow and, if so, how? Oh God, how she wishes she hadn't fallen asleep, so she could have seen it for herself. She makes a quick mental note to review the tapes and recordings with a fine-toothed comb to see if any of this has registered or been recorded.

But back to the moment at hand. "Bethany, what is your friend telling you right now?" Liz inquires. "Well, she says she doesn't like this place very much and wants to go back but doesn't know how." Oh great, Liz thinks to herself. What do I do now? Before she can come to any conclusions, a voice suggests she contact Stephan. What? Who's saying that?

The voice answers in a more demanding manner. I am! Call Stephan! As Liz searches the room, first in one direction, then in the next to determine the source of the voice, her eyes slowly rest upon the hybrid, whose crystal blue eyes yield that it is the source. "Okay, okay. I'm dialing.... I'm dialing" Liz obeys.

Thank God for speed dialing, as Liz's shaking hands are just barely able to hold onto her cell phone that she miraculously remembered to take from her office and put in her lab jacket pocket.

After what seems like a million rings, Stephan answers... "Hi, I thought you weren't going to call me until the morning..." Liz stutters, "S-S-Stephan? S-S-Stephan? Y-you're not going to believe this..."

Liz makes every attempt to recount the events exactly as they happened to her husband who is now totally silent on the other end of the phone. "Stephan, this being..." Bethany interrupts... "Daphne!" "Sorry", Liz interjects "Daphne...told me to call you. Isn't that interesting?" she continues in a panicked high-toned voice."

"Stephan, I need you down here now! I've got this alien hybrid...excuse me, Daphne...with us and I don't know what to do!" Stephan finally breaks his silence and tells Liz to hold on, that he's on his way. Hold on? Hold on? Just what am I supposed to hold on to? Liz humors to herself. Forgetting that the hybrid can read thought, it responds to Liz by assuring her that Stephan will have an answer to their dilemma. She hopes, Daphne - is it?... is right.

Liz abruptly ends her frantic conversation and prays that Stephan can get there without killing himself or, just as importantly, not being followed by Byron Huxley or any of his cohorts.

Byron Huxley is a bit of an eccentric but also well-known for his deep pockets, philanthropic endeavors not to be overshadowed by his entrepreneurial prowess earning him the well-deserved financial reputation most well aligned with political influence at the highest level. But Stephan has recently learned of the darker side of Mr. Huxley and his connection with the secret government's Black Op and the long- held Truth Embargo the government has fostered concerning the U.F.O and E.T. presence.

As the only registered U.F.O. lobbyist in the world, Stephan has been trying to obtain an audience with the renowned billionaire; but be careful what you wish for, as Stephan learned in a private meeting with this auspicious figure a few short weeks ago.

As it turned out, Huxley uncovered Stephan's "other identity" and of his connection and interaction with off-planet beings – specifically, the alien hybrids.

Byron Huxley revealed to Stephan that he was dying from a rare form of brain cancer, one that had no known treatment, recourse or cure. Knowing of Stephan's connection to the hybrids, he proposed that he act as liaison on his behalf in the hope that with either their medical technology to cure his disease or, at the very least, get him to their planet or star system hopping to retard his ultimate fate. In exchange, Huxley would "ensure" success in whatever political entreaty he chose. Tempting to say the least. However, after a long week of weighing the options, Stephan turned Huxley's generous offer down. Huxley was not pleased with this decision.

And so it is, that Stephan is sure that he is being watched closely by Huxley and his henchmen and has trepidation, bordering on paranoia with every new element that crosses his path regarding the hybrids. So, is it any wonder that the level of his anxiety has reached an all-time high with Liz's urgent phone call?

Finally reaching the parking lot by Liz's lab, Stephan turns off his headlights and drives his car around to the rear entrance to Liz's office, continually glancing into his rearview mirror to see if the car that appeared to be following him since he left the house was anywhere in sight. It is not.

Dismissing the cloak and dagger suspicion, Stephan still can't seem to shake the feeling that he is being followed. He vows to use more caution when talking on the phone or driving his car - just in case.

Stephan enters the lobby of the office building and takes the elevator up to the second floor suites that house Liz's office and the sleep lab.

Once inside, he gingerly walks to the lab and opens the door quietly so as not to disturb the mood that awaits within. The room is dark, except for the dim light that emits from within the dome structure. Liz had her team install a controllable lighting system to produce the desired reduction of light in an effort to assist the subject into a relaxed state.

Liz spies Stephan in her peripheral vision as he enters the room and silently says a Thank you, God! under her breath. At that moment, the hybrid cocks its head in her direction and telepathically asks, what is the origin of that word - God?

Before Liz can worry about an answer, Stephan approaches her side and places a reassuring arm about her waist as he gazes inside the glass dome that encases Bethany and the hybrid, who are now in an upright-seated position. He, too, is taken aback not just by the hybrid's very presence, but its oversized, strikingly blue, crystal eyes that permeate his very being. He can't help but notice that even though they are all part of this unusual gathering, Bethany and the hybrid are each holding an arm of the stuffed rabbit just like most children would do under normal circumstances. But this is anything but normal.

Stephan stands in silence for a few moments and telepathically greets the hybrid. Within moments Stephan lets out a loud laugh as he relays what the hybrid has shared with him, which is how funny our species looks and how archaic our method of travel is, referring to his need to drive a car to get over here. Funny, indeed.

As Liz, Stephan and, especially, Bethany share telepathic communication, there is no need for Stephan to translate the internal dialog that's going on between he and the hybrid any longer. Everyone gets it.

Bethany speaks aloud: "She just wants to go home! Can you help her? I want my Mommy! Can I go home now, too?"

Liz is well aware of how this must be affecting Bethany but doesn't want to remove her from the dome until they figure out what to do with the hybrid, who obviously has an attachment with Bethany and might display some negative behavior should they be separated.

"Stephan, I have an idea." Liz quips; "But we're going to have to work fast." Stephan is all ears and gives her the go-ahead signal.

"What if we have both Bethany and her little friend, here, lay back down and think about Daphne's returning home. Remember, they got here through thought...why wouldn't it work in reverse?" Stephan nods in agreement, but questions Liz on why the hybrid demanded his presence, if it's just that simple? Before Liz can answer his question, the hybrid tells them - I needed to see you both, as together you will be instrumental in my evolution. I do not have clearance to speak further. Just know that all is as it should be. I'm ready to leave, now.

With that, Liz instructs Bethany to lie down and as she does so, the hybrid follows her action. Both Liz and Stephan begin to move away from the dome, but Stephan hesitates, as he pulls out the digital camera from his jacket pocket and quickly takes a random shot of the dome without aiming in the hopes he's captured this most unusual setting.

Once backed away from the apparatus, Liz reaches for the lab's console and slowly dims the lighting inside the dome to almost full blackout. She quietly instructs both Bethany and the hybrid to relax and dream. As Liz closely watches the monitors that record the brain waive activity, she is relieved to see that Bethany, at least, has reached Delta state and is, indeed sleeping.

In deafening silence Stephan and Liz peer into the darkness as they wait for some indication that the hybrid has reached transition and is, once again, returned to its own state of being.

Within moments they get the confirmation they seek when Bethany shouts from out of the blackness, "Goodbye! Thanks for coming...Can I go home now?"

THE DILEMA

*L*ittle did I realize at the time, but my sleep over at Liz's lab was about to become a major breakthrough in studying what happens to the brain during different levels of sleep and would be hailed as groundbreaking on all levels. Not only had Liz designed a state-of-the art conduit that would monitor and record my dream state but bore actual witness to and clinical confirmation of my claims of interdimensional travel and interaction with hybrids. This was huge!

Now, you have to understand, that my mother wasn't aware of what happened that night until several weeks later when I wigged out one night about wanting to see my hybrid friend, I called Daphne…"I want to see Daphne…NOW!"

My mom struggled to calm my hysterics and questioned me over and over about "Who is this Daphne person?" Person? Um…not exactly. I think I may have even giggled out loud a bit, mid-tirade, when she asked me that one.

I do recall, clearly, my little brother Ryan sitting on the floor of our shared bedroom in open-mouthed horror as I began spinning my tale of going to the play house while the rest of the family slept; and how enthusiastically I rambled on about spending time with little children that had over sized heads, large black, slanted eyes and only three fingers; (I never did get to the part about them not having a perceivable mouth or ears), but I think my mom was getting the picture.

Before my mom could openly react to all this foolishness, Ryan intuitively bolted, as fast as his little feet could carry him, to the corner of our bedroom, crouched down and covered his ears with his tiny hands, squeezing his eyes tightly shut, most *likely wishing I'd shut the heck up and stop this ill-advised disclosure. But too late... for continue on, I did, in full force and in technicolor!*

I'm not exactly sure how, but I think this mayhem began to wind down when my mom promised me that she would call Liz to see what she could do to help me get in contact with ..."What's her name again? Daphne, is it?"

After wiping my tear-streaked face with her now trembling hands, mom kissed me on the top of my head, stroked my hair, then instructed both Ryan and I to stay in our room until further notice...her voice all but a whisper by the tail end of her words, as she unsteadily stood up and left the room.

In a flash she was downstairs. I shot a glance at Ryan, who by now, had come back from his purposeful exile, then heard mom's inaudible mumbling; her heavy- footed pacing provided the evidence of her own hysteria as she dialed the phone, to who, I had no idea. And that was that.

(Flashback)

Liz sits at her home office desk pouring over and over the data from Bethany's sleep study, that took place a couple of weeks before. Because Liz and Stephan had been gone for that time period meeting with Brad Tanner, a UFO expert of sorts in Sedona, Arizona, she'd not been able to meet with her team nor seen Bethany in person since that fateful night.

Liz's mind is spinning in every direction possible...I need to consult with my team and get my dissertation ready to present before the scientific and medical communities, and then jumps to... Hopefully this will get published in the Journal of Psychiatry

& Neuroscience and who knows...maybe the journal of the American Medical Association!

Ego aside, Liz realizes how she's just achieved and, more importantly, recorded Bethany's amazing sleep study, which would undoubtedly not only put her name on the tongue of every researcher in this field of endeavor, but what a powerful impact this would have on the exploration of interdimensional interaction!

Liz mentally jumps to her need to formulate a post-study evaluation with Bethany on how all this is affecting her and if this interaction with the hybrid, referred to as Daphne, could be controlled. She wondered; *Would it mean that we could literally send out an invitation to them to pay us a visit, or, are WE the ones who'd be granted an audience?*

What concerns Liz the most is Bethany. Since she's kept in close touch with Bethany's mom while she was away, she still can't help but feel a bit paranoid about Rachel's less than enthusiastic responses inquiring about Bethany's post-sleep study demeanor.

Rachel did make it quite clear that the only reason she even allowed Bethany to partake in the sleep study was in hope this would end all this nonsense and for Liz to just "fix" whatever the problem was and make it all go away.

So, now Liz has the monumental challenge of spoon-feeding Rachel with the concept that her five-year old daughter has the ability to physically manifest a being from another dimension and see just how badly will this information freak her out? What do *you* think?

Realizing she can't put off calling Rachel any longer, Liz reluctantly reaches for the phone but is startled by the ring of an incoming call, almost dropping it from her anxious, vice-gripped hands.

"Hello?" Liz answers. There is a long silence with no response, so Liz repeats, "Hello? Anybody there?" Again, met with silence.

Liz was just about to hang up when she hears, "Dr. Wolf? Dr. Wolf...this is Rachel...Rachel Wilcox, Bethany's mom...um... sorry to bother you...but we need to talk."

Liz is immediately concerned and a bit alarmed, as any sentence that includes "...we need to talk..." can't be good. Liz jumps right in and gets to the point, "Hi Rachel, is Bethany alright? Is everything okay?"

For what seems like an eternity, Rachel finally answers with a firmer response, "Well, actually no, it's not! I'm calling to tell you that she won't be coming to your office for any more of those damn sessions!"

Totally caught off guard, Liz's mind is racing in a million directions trying to comprehend what she is hearing and prepares to do damage control for...what? She hasn't a clue.

"Rachel, I'm so sorry that you're upset. But you need to tell me what this is all about, so I can understand and perhaps do something to ease your anger. Please, tell me what's wrong" Liz pleads.

"I'm going to be brutally honest with you, Dr. Wolf... the only reason I brought Bethany to you in the first place is because all the other doctors wouldn't touch her...they thought she was suffering from some post traumatic event, even inferred that my husband and I might be guilty of some sort of inappropriate behavior with our own daughter...can you imagine that?" Liz remains silent.

"Well, I knew my Bethany just needed to get some of her crazy notions about playing with imaginary aliens out of her head and since you came highly recommended...and seeing whereas you worked with kids that talk about stuff like this...well, we just naturally believed that you could help. But never, ever did I think that you'd actually make things worse!" by now Rachel is sobbing uncontrollably.

Liz quickly concludes that Bethany must have told her mother about the hybrid, Daphne, appearing next to her the night of the sleep study then asks, "I gather that Bethany has shared the remarkable event that happened that evening..." Before Liz can utter another word, Rachel yells into the phone, "EVENT? That event, if it even happened at all, has my daughter crying for someone named Daphne and how she can't see her anymore! What the hell went on that night, Dr. Wolf? I need to know..."

"Rachel, I want you to calm down. I'll be happy to tell you everything, but you need to take a deep breath and calm down." Liz's mind immediately races to Bethany's state of mind, so asks, "How is Bethany doing? I really must talk with her, Rachel. I need to know what she means that she can't see Daphne (she caught herself before slipping and using the word "hybrid", which surely would cause a more catastrophic meltdown) ... anymore? I can meet you at the office right away."

Liz can hear Rachel still sniffing on the other end of the phone and continues to plead for a meeting at the office as soon as possible. Reluctantly, Rachel agrees, but on one condition, that she will be right there in the room when Bethany is questioned. Oh God! Liz thinks to herself. She was hoping to have Bethany all to herself so that they could talk openly as before, but it was not to be.

"Okay, Rachel... of course you can sit in. I'll meet you and Bethany at my office in twenty minutes?" With that Rachel confirms that they'll both be there, but warns, "If any of that funny stuff goes on, I'm taking my daughter out of there and reporting you to the authorities. Putting crazy ideas into an innocent child's head...I mean of all the..." then she hangs up.

Liz grabs her car keys and heads for the door, her mind whirling out of control. "Focus, Liz, focus!" she shouts to herself. There is so much riding on how effectively she handles this crisis that her head feels like it will literally explode any minute.

The drive over to the office finds Liz riddled with nervous energy, which she knows she must harness by the time she meets with Rachel and Bethany.

As Liz pulls into the parking lot, she is grateful that she is the first to arrive and quickly exits the car and heads up to her office. Once she enters the inner sanctum, she feels a sense of calm come over her while she turns on the lights and reaches for Bethany's file that, ironically is on top of a pile of records that she wanted to review.

Grateful that she has these few moments to go over Bethany's file, Liz stops only long enough to utter a private prayer that Rachel will allow Bethany's sessions to continue, as this is a crucial time in her therapy and one that Liz feels could result in less than desirable results, if interrupted so abruptly. Liz hears the outer office door open and whispers to herself, Okay, here we go!

"Hi Liz", Bethany acknowledges in a less than enthusiastic tone while her mother's stern expression tells it all. "Well, hi there, yourself, Ms. Bethany! I've missed you while I was away. How are you doing?" Liz attempts to not let Bethany feel the tension that engulfs the room, but decides to keep it real, after all…this is Bethany, the wonder child who probably knows more than any room full of adults.

"Hey there, kiddo, what do you say…you, Mommy and I go into my office and visit for a bit? How does that sound?"

"Okay" Bethany says with a sigh. "Can I draw some pictures?" she perks up a bit when asking the question. "I don't see why not…Mom? Okay with you?"

Rachel nods her head in agreement as they all move into the session room to sit. Liz walks over to her desk and discretely reaches into a desk drawer to turn on the tape recorder, catching Rachel's eye indicating that she is doing so. Rachel nods again and let's Liz takes the lead.

"So, Bethany... what's been going on since the last time I saw you? Mommy tells me that you've been a bit upset. Want to tell me about it?" Normally, Bethany is a chatterbox at this juncture but with her mother sitting in, appears to hesitate slightly before she begins to recount for Liz: "Well, I'm mad at Daphne..." Liz prods her on, "Why? Did she do something to upset you?" Bethany's eyes dart in the direction of her mother then back at Liz, then shyly looks down and answers, "Yes. Yes, she upset me..."

Before Liz can ask why, Bethany gets emotional and begins to blurt out, "Because she won't play with me anymore! She told me she doesn't want to play with me anymore!" she cries.

Liz reaches for a tissue and hands it to Rachel to wipe Bethany's tears then urges her to go on: "Remember how Daphne and I would play at the play house...then she came to play here...that night? Well, she got really mad when she had to leave and got into a lot of trouble because she came to play with me, here...the night I slept over...remember?"

Softly Liz says, "Yes, I remember...go on." "Well", Bethany continues, "Mommy and Daddy didn't know that Daphne came to play and when I told them about it, THEY got mad, too!" Now Bethany is in full hysterics. "I don't want Daphne to go away! I want to play with her...and the others...why can't I play with them anymore?"

Liz, now facing Rachel, asks her how she feels about all this, hoping that she'll remember to be careful with her choice of words while in Bethany's presence, "I...we...her father and I never asked Bethany what went on during your sessions with her. We were always advised to let that be between you and her...so, you can imagine our...surprise when Bethany shared her 'experience' with... Daphne, is it?"

Liz now has a full grasp on Rachel's outrage that's clearly born out of fear and lack of knowledge. She tries to use another tact, "Rachel, I want to apologize for keeping you out of the loop about my sessions with Bethany. I realize now that was unfair and it's no wonder that you were...freaked out by what you heard."

Liz knows that the next words out of mouth had better be good ones, or she'll lose Bethany as her special patient. But it goes far beyond that. Bethany has become so much more than that to Liz and she has always tried to let her know that and hoped that Rachel knew it, too.

"Rachel, I would like to suggest that you and your husband come to see me, alone, so that we can talk about all this and perhaps you'll feel more comfortable with Bethany continuing her sessions with me."

Liz needs to get across to Rachel how imperative it is for Bethany to continue, especially now. It doesn't matter at this point what Rachel and her husband believe about all this, because, quite frankly, they may never understand the unique and special talents their daughter possesses. However, Liz is determined to at least educate them slowly into the possibilities of their child's interaction with beings from...well...not here. God help me! she prays to herself.

Liz begins again, "Rachel, wouldn't you agree that since Bethany and I have been having our little 'chats' that she has been happy and on target?" "Yes..." Rachel replies. Good!

Liz thinks and continues... "And wouldn't you agree that her mood swings and outburst have decreased, if not ceased all together in the months that we've been meeting?" "Yes..." Rachel was weakening.

Bring it on home, Liz, "And while this latest event was a bit of a shock to you, wouldn't you agree that Bethany's interaction with...um...Daphne is extremely important to her and to disallow it at this time could be detrimental?" "Yes, I agree." Rachel acquiesced. Success!

"Bethany, how would you like to continue coming to see me and together perhaps we can figure out how to talk with Daphne to see if you can play again? Okay?" Bethany brightens, looks at her mother and pleads, "I want to Mommy! Can I? Can I, please...PLEASE?"

"Okay, Bethany, okay, sweetie." Rachel then turns to Liz with tears in her eyes as Bethany heads for the door and softly speaks to Liz, "I'm sorry I got so mad...I'm just so scared. I just don't understand any of this...but I'll try. I really will try..."

With that, Liz gives Rachel a reassuring hug and tells her to speak with her husband and let her know when it would be convenient for them to all meet. She also reminds her of how special Bethany is to her, especially now, that she's about to become a mother, herself.

Rachel's mood turns from somber to joy as she shrieks "You are? Oh, Dr. Wolf, that's great!"

"Please, call me Liz", she says to Rachel. "Liz, it is."

Once Bethany and Rachel leave the office, Liz sits down behind her desk to shut off the tape recorder, then stares off into nowhere uttering her words of gratitude to whoever is listening, "Thank you...*Thank you...*"

KRYSTAL

*I*t's *funny how promises made sometimes can never be kept,
even with the best of intentions. What I'm talking about was
my mother's promise to me, and to Liz, who had just performed
an amazing sleep study that would forever change the way
science perceived what happens during our non-awake hours.
Mom let her own fears govern her inability to follow through
with a promise to let me continue my visits with Liz and keep
this sleep study going. It was simply too much for her.*

*I knew for a fact that my father didn't agree with her decision
because I often heard them "discussing" it, in not so soft tones
with one another. But in the end, Mom won out.*

*All I knew was that I couldn't see Liz anymore but, even more
devastating, was that I believed I'd never see Daphne again, for
my time in the play house had come to an abrupt halt after that
fateful night in the lab when Daphne came to visit. I was beyond
heartbroken. Those visits were over. Done!*

*I cried a lot and pleaded with my mother to let me visit with
Liz, but she always had an excuse like, Liz was out of town, or
Liz was sick. I knew intuitively none of that was true and yet,
how could I question my own mother's motives? For deep down
in my heart I knew my Mom wanted only what was best for
me...she just didn't know, what I knew.*

*I spent many a night trying my darnedest to reconnect to the
"other side" with the hope that I could continue my magical
journey to the play house and frolic with Daphne and all the
others, including The Keeper. But it was over...or so I thought.*

(Flashback)

It's been three years since the groundbreaking sleep study with Bethany, Liz and Daphne; and yet seems like just yesterday to Bethany, who is about to turn eight-years old in a few days.

As a special surprise, Rachel whisks Bethany off for a Mother/Daughter day of shopping and eating at one of her favorite restaurant chains, complete with and outdoor play area.

Rachel and Bethany select an outside picnic style table to enjoy the sunshine and embrace the warm Spring temperatures that urge people to the great outdoors.

"I'm going to place our order, honey. What do you want to drink?" Rachel questions. "Oh, I don't care...wait! I want a thick chocolate milkshake with colored sprinkles on it!" "Oh Bethany..." her mother chides. "But it does sound delicious. Okay, I'll be right back", Rachel teases as she stands before the outside ordering counter, while Bethany slowly ambles over to the play area, idly gazing at nothing in particular.

"Hi Bethany!" a very young child's voice shouts in delight as she approaches, running at a full clip. A bewildered Bethany, bolts upright at this unfamiliar person's enthusiastic advance. Then, within a micro-second, a recognition; those eyes, those piercing blue eyes..."Daphne?...DAPHNE!" Bethany screams in delight as the two fall into one another's arms in a choking embrace.

Oblivious to all that surrounds them, the girls giggle wildly, all the while prattling on, talking over one another as they profess how much they've missed being together.

However, their magical reunion is short lived when a tall man, obviously the young girl's father, approaches and breaks the spell correcting Bethany, "Hi, there young lady. You must be mistaken...this is my daughter, Krystal. She's three years old... well, almost four, actually. How old are you?"

Bethany is quick to recognize the father as Stephan Wolf, Liz's husband whom she had met several times and last seen the night of the sleep study. Her head begins to spin as her brain attempts to formulate the words she is about to speak.

"Hi, Mr. Wolf. Don't you remember me? It's Bethany...I used to visit with Liz...Boy, I sure miss her."

Now it's Stephan's turn to be a bit unsteady as he struggles with - should he tell Bethany of Liz's untimely passing shortly after giving birth to their daughter, Krystal, but decides not to mention it at all.

When he recovers and looks more closely, Stephan surely does recognize Bethany and gives her a big hug. "Well, you've certainly grown a lot since I last saw you. Is your Mom here with here with you?", Stephan asks with a full-on grin. He makes note of how the girls continue their embrace; one arm about each other's shoulders while their free hands hold on tightly to one another during the entire exchange.

Bethany points over to where her mother, Rachel, has just picked up their food and drink order. Rachel, spies the trio and wonders who Bethany is talking to, then waves her free hand indicating that her lunch is ready.

Bethany returns an acknowledging gesture then resumes her conversation; "Krystal? Why do you call her Krystal? No, her name is Daphne...don't you remember? Don't you remember the night I slept over at Liz's office and Daphne came to visit? Boy, were we surprised, huh?"

Stephan definitely does remember that night, quite clearly, in fact. By now Stephan observes Krystal and Bethany as they appear to be "exchanging" conversation without words, a process that Stephan is quite familiar with, himself. Bethany begins to giggle and then says aloud, "Oh Daphne, you're so funny. You still don't know how to say some things with words, do you?"

With that, Bethany's Mom calls for her once again to come sit down to eat her lunch. Realizing that she has no more time to talk, Bethany quickly turns to Stephan and asks, "Mr. Wolf, can Daphne come to play at my house some time? Now that she's... um...here?", then rattles off her telephone number hoping he'll remember it.

Stephan thinks for but a moment as he connects the dots in his own mind, then looks into his daughters beautiful, piercing, crystal blue eyes and answers, "On one condition...you call her Krystal." For which Bethany replies ... "See you soon... Krystal!", she promises, as she turns to join her mother. See you soon...

DANGER...STRANGER!

*I*n lieu of my sessions with Liz, my father convinced my mom
to pursue an alternate course of treatment for my 'condition'
by enrolling me at a private school for children who exhibited
unusual abilities, or were considered 'gifted', (not that my mother
thought my talents and abilities were anything like a gift... quite
the opposite!)

Many of the other kid's abilities ranged anywhere from
incredibly high academics, musical prodigies and then there
were children like me, who demonstrated extreme high levels
of psychic capabilities; some of which boasted interaction with
beings from other dimensions. We were affectionately known
as "The Woo-Woo Kids", a label that didn't attach itself to
what would normally be perceived as negative and so the other
children simply left us alone. Because they didn't fit into the
status quo themselves, they simply accepted that our "talents"
were different, plain and simple. Now, that's not to say that they
understood what we could do or, better yet, believed for a second
that any of it was real. It just was what it was to them...weird!

For the most part, we "Woo-Woo Kids" hung out with one
another pretty exclusively, not that there were a lot of us, (six
or so, I remember). We only ventured out of our familiar clique
every now and then to interact with the Brainiac's, typically
when we felt like deliberately provoking them into any reaction
we could get; especially when we'd share our experiences with
aliens or doing "readings" on them, just for the sheer fun of it.

A psychic reading of an individual is a specific way to discern
information received through the use of heightened perceptive
abilities; or natural extensions of the basic human senses of

sight, sound, touch, taste and instinct. Everyone has this ability, but others, like me, have won the psychic lottery and have a ton of it. Not always the blessing one might think.

Look at it this way, some people who play the piano can only play "Chopsticks", while others can play Chopin or Mozart. The degree of their ability is what makes the difference and, I might add, if the talent is properly nourished and encouraged, there's no limit to the heights you can achieve.

While the school was well-known and revered for its unique student population, it was also the target for controversy between the religious and the scientific communities- at-large. The religious groups viewed the encouragement of psychic abilities as blasphemy which went against every belief that they held most dear, gleaned from the millennium of bible teachings. They also thought it exceedingly arrogant that anyone, other than God him/her-self, would even dare to suggest they had this kind of supreme power and ability to "know" the future.

Then there was the clandestine Black Op element that held the potential to rule the world, working closely with alien beings whose own suspicious agenda jeopardized the very fiber of our human existence. 'Kids like us' were sought after by these covert operations at a frightening rate, to explore our level of possible communication and interaction with the unseen beings that have walked among us since time began.

So, as you can imagine, the unfolding of all this underground activity and interest in me became confusing, if not overwhelming. I needed to identify and discern the good guys from the bad guys...not always an easy task...even for me!

✧ (Flashback)

He sits in silent, controlled, patience in the rear seat of the shiny black town car. The chauffeur's head, body and eyes remain robotically riveted forward, daring only a hasty glance at his passenger via the rearview mirror. The passenger grumbles inaudible words under his breath as he stares intently at the brick and mortar school building across the street that is surrounded by twelve-foot high chain linked fencing. He sits waiting... patiently waiting.

For the past three weeks, both driver and passenger find themselves in the exact same spot at the precise hour; the sound of the school bell breaks the silence bringing the passenger to full attention. He brings laser focus on each child as they burst forth from the duel glass and metal doors that lead out to the playground, eager to take advantage of their short recess period.

"There!", the passenger emits aloud... "There she is!" Reaching for the car door handle, the passenger slowly, but deliberately exits the car, his pale skin and frail body leave no question that this being is struggling to remain upright. His grave illness now overrides his chronological years, leaving the appearance of a man far older than he is.

The chauffeur lowers his window and begins to question the man about his choice to exit the car, but is waived off with an abrupt hand gesture, leaving no doubt about him carrying out his intention...the time has arrived for the introduction.

Bethany joins her friends running around the school playground in their revelry, then suddenly stops dead in her tracks. She lifts her face to the sky as if listening to something unheard by others, then sharply pivots her body to face the approaching figure who continues his measured course toward the chain linked fence...

his destination now crystal clear. He feigns a smile as he draws nearer to where she stands entranced; equating his stride to that of a lion stalking its prey.

Her first instinct is to run in the opposite direction and alert one of the recess chaperons of this man's presence, but does not. Seeing that Bethany remains in place rather than fleeing, the man relaxes his smile and calls her name loudly enough for her to hear but goes unnoticed by the others.

Feeling somewhat secure behind the fence and knowing full well that she could scream for help at any time, Bethany slowly approaches the fence where the man now stands, fingers locked between the fence's links, most likely to support of his weakened body.

"Hello, Bethany...I'm so happy to meet you. My name is Byron Huxley and I am an ....um...er...acquaintance of Liz Tanner Wolf and her husband, Stephan, whom I know you meet with now and then to discuss...ah...let's say...visits with your little friends?"

Bethany tilts her head in one direction then in another in an effort to read who this man is and what does he want. She doesn't have to wait long to find out.

"Bethany, I know how wonderfully smart you are and that you have...um...special abilities. I'd like to talk with you about helping me with a little project I'm involved with...using your...uh...talents?" Bethany, indicates her continued wariness of this man with furrowed brow, and is about to speak but Byron Huxley detects that he's caught the attention of a female chaperon who is hastily headed in their direction; so, he decides to cease this line of conversation stating that he'd like to chat with her again at another time...if she'd like. Bethany does not answer.

With the chaperon now calling out, "Excuse me sir...Can I help you?" Byron Huxley lifts his hand from the support of the fence and gestures an unspoken No, that's Okay, then turns his infirmed body and sluggishly heads back to the sleek black haven of the vehicle.

Once the chaperon reaches Bethany's side, she places an arm about Bethany's tiny shoulder in demonstration to the man, who by now has re-entered the luxury car, that this child is well watched and protected. Still keeping a steeled eye on the man, the chaperon inquires, "Bethany, who was that man? Do you know him? You know you're not supposed to talk to strangers, dear?"…Bethany chuckles to herself inside, (*if she only knew!*)

"Come on", the chaperon urges Bethany, "…recess is almost over. Go find your friends." Normally full of chatter, this time Bethany oddly chooses not to answer any of the chaperon's questions. The unspoken reason Bethany felt assured that no harm will befall her, is not because there is a twelve-foot high chain linked fence between she and Byron Huxley but more due to the looming ghostly shadowed, rubbery hand that held hers the whole time. She finds confidant comfort in knowing that The Keepers' presence throughout the whole encounter was visible only to her…or so she thought.

There is one child, an older boy named Jarred, who intently watches as Bethany slowly drops her tiny hand from that of the three- fingered being and hurries back to find her friends who are totally oblivious to what has just occurred. She gives one final glance over her shoulder as the vehicle slowly pulls away. She's not seen the last of Mr. Huxley…nor Jarred.

THE DARKER SIDE OF LIGHT

*L*ooking back on my early childhood, I considered myself to be a happy-go-lucky little kid. Energetic, playful, imaginative and often, more than not to the chagrin of my parents, mischievous. But all in all, I was a well behaved, kind and compassionate member of our clan.

Along with being viewed as a 'gifted child', came a treasure trove of expectations from both my family members and the world of scholastic academics. But as time would prove out, being a kid like me, who possessed the gifts of clairvoyance (a supernatural ability to perceive events in the future); clairaudience (able to hear things that others cannot); along with remote viewing (meaning I could physically remain in one geographic location while my mind traveled to another targeted location, widely taught and used for military surveillance); and an extremely high level of psychic communication, carried with it a whole other need to acquire a unique set of coping skills...for everyone involved.

Now add to that the exclusive ability to traverse between dimensions and interact with humanoid hybrids – ensured a colossal formula for disaster!

It was more than enough that I had to deal with my family and teachers keeping a close eye on my activities and behavior. But now there appeared to be a heightened interest from secret governments around the globe that were desperate to learn more about a kid who had the ability to interact with off planet beings -so it shouldn't have been a surprise to anyone that, suddenly, there was an onslaught of desperation to get to this kid - Me!

But there was more...for there also existed a select sub-set of malevolent individuals in the private sector of equal suspicious agenda. And, if the truth be known, they were to be feared almost as much, if not more so – for they had more at stake than the leaders of the foreign countries...their own personal survival. I'm talking about Byron Huxley, a formidable man of vast wealth and great influence who would "encourage" those in political power to do his bidding by utilizing his financial persuasion in exchange for these favors; a lesson I was about to learn, the hard way.

(Flashback)

Mid-week activities are status quo in the Wilcox household with Bethany and her siblings going about their daily lives between, school, play-dates and after school sporting practices. Rachel's day, however, was about to become a bit more chaotic as she answers the irritating ringing of the telephone.

"Hello", Rachel declares, somewhat annoyed as her laundry burdened hands fumble with the phone's receiver. "Hi Honey", the voice on the other end responds. "Larry, what's up? I'm really busy sweetie...", Rachel pleads. "Well, I just wanted to give you a heads up that I'm bringing a client home for dinner tonight..."

Not waiting for any further explanation, Rachel lets out an exasperated "Really, Larry? Of all days...the house is a mess - I don't have the right food in the house to simply 'whip up' a fabulous feast for whomever this guest is that warrants such short notice, and..." at this point Larry gently interrupts his wife's escalating protests. "Rach, this is a new, very important client that I was asked to host for the evening. He has a ton of financial investments that need our professional management, so my boss asked me, personally, to dazzle this client with a home cooked meal. I couldn't say no, especially since my review is right around the corner and I'm in line for a huge promotion. I need this Rach..."

Rachel wishes she could argue her point further but knows how paramount this is for her husband's career and in the end, the family's financial security so, she lets out an audible sigh of surrender. "OK, Larry, but let me go as now I've got to run to the grocery store to pick up some food for this 'dazzling dinner'. Got any special requests?"

"Nah, I know you'll find something fabulous...always do." Rachel is no stranger to Larry's last minute 'guess who's coming to dinner' requests, just wasn't in the mood to help with the 'dog and pony' show this particular day. "Okay, honey. But give me some time to put things in order, will ya? Dinner at 6:30?" "You got it, girl! Thanks Rach...love you..." Rachel smiles as she returns, "Love you more!" before hanging up.

Rachel catches eldest son, Charlie, just as he's about to head out the kitchen door to parts unknown, and tells him that he's on sibling duty while she runs out to the store to pick up supplies for the evening's unexpected dinner guest. Ignoring his moans and groans in obvious objection, Rachel grabs her purse and car keys, blows an air kiss to her children then heads out the door completely focused on her assigned mission.

In record time, Rachel returns with delicacies piled high inside her shopping bags and gives herself a boastful smirk in the car's rearview mirror before exiting and whispers aloud to no one in particular...If *THIS* doesn't 'dazzle" Mr. Money Bags then I don't know what will!

Rachel decides to feed the children a small snack late in the afternoon so as to hold them off for the formal sit down with their father's guest. Shortly thereafter, she makes sure the children are dressed in fresh clothing, hair preened, house vacuumed, dusted and polished; table is set with their finest dinner and glassware, topped off with crystal candle holders that are heirlooms from her great grandmother. Rachel places a colorful array of freshly picked flowers from their garden at the table's center as the last finishing touch, then steps back to admire her creation. "Doesn't get any homier than this", she mumbles to herself, then adds, "Show time!"

At the appointed hour, Larry's voice heralds their arrival as he and his guest enter through the modest home's front door. One by one the troops fall into place in the foyer for inspection and to greet the honored guest.

Once Larry cordially ushers in the mystery guest, without warning, Bethany emits an audible gasp, standing frozen to the foyer floor; Ryan stares silently with bulging eyes, his mouth agape, while Charlie lowers his head letting out a perceptible WOW!

Larry has neglected to forewarn Rachel of this guest's frail physical condition, jaundiced skin and yellowing eyes, evidencing his obvious grave illness. She can only hope that her shock at seeing his discernable malady doesn't show and that the children's shuddered reaction to his appearance goes unnoticed. It does not.

Shutting the front door, Larry is aware of his family's unexpected response to his guest's entrance, uneasily clears his throat and begins the introduction: "Everyone, I'd like you meet Mr. Byron Huxley. Mr. Huxley is thinking about doing business with the firm I work for and so I thought it would be nice for him to join us for dinner and relax a bit while he's in town."

Bethany is horrified! She knows this man – she remembers this man...she doesn't like this man! She immediately steps back behind her brother, Charlie, who extends an awkward handshake in response to his father's raised eyebrow prompting.

Thinking that her daughter is simply being shy, or intimidated by Huxley's deathlike façade, Rachel encourages Bethany to step forward and greet Mr. Huxley properly, which she does, ever so reluctantly. Ryan, somewhat oblivious to what the others are reacting to, watches his sister closely and tries to tune into her trepidation about this stranger who has come into their home. All Ryan knows is that his sister doesn't like this man and that's enough for him.

Excuses are made about the younger children's hesitancy and glossed over, as Rachel announces that dinner is about ready and asks Larry to usher Mr. Huxley to the dining room table. Bryon Huxley makes grand statements about the room's lovely appointments and is offered to take a seat…right next to Bethany, with Charlie and Ryan seated directly across the table.

Ryan remains fixated on his sister's wide-eyed horror and attempts to catch her attention in an effort to begin their special telepathic exchange in the hopes of getting some answers about this man she seems to be so afraid of. Bethany, on the other hand, deliberately keeps her gaze downward for she knows of Ryan's attempts and is fearful of connecting with him sharing what she knows of this man. For Ryan will surely speak her thoughts aloud, a faux pas he's done in the past, which would be a bad thing… a very bad thing …for everyone.

The meal is brought to the table and the dinner conversations turn to mundane subjects that include the children's education and activities. Bethany pushes her food about her plate, not once partaking of even a morsel, hoping the dinner will be over soon so she can retreat to the sanctity of her bedroom and away from this man.

All throughout dinner, the three siblings exchange micro-glances at one another, eyes darting back and forth, stuttering reluctant answers when asked to join in conversation with their guest.

After what seems like an excruciatingly long dinner, Rachel asks her children to help clear the table for which Bethany is the first to bolt out of her seat in compliance of her mother's request. Once all is cleared, the grownups head for the comfort of the living room, so Bethany gratefully assumes she can remove herself from Mr. Huxley's presence. At least that is her hope until… "Bethany…" Larry voices, "Bethany, why don't you and Ryan take Mr. Huxley out into our backyard before it gets too dark and show him the lovely flower garden you and your brother helped Mommy plant, while I help her make coffee and get ready to serve dessert?

Before Bethany can object, Bryon Huxley deadlocks his eyes with hers while gesturing for her to lead the way. Bethany again thinks of her brother Ryan and his propensity to blurt out all that he knows and so nervously agrees and offers, "I don't think Ry-Ry would enjoy it very much Daddy, but I can do it by myself…" her voice trails off.

"Grab a sweater, sweetie, as it's starting to get a little chilly out there", Rachel instructs her daughter while carrying the last of the dinner plates to the kitchen.

A very unwilling Bethany is first to step out into the family's well-manicured back yard and heads directly to one of many small blooming gardens right outside the dining room slider, providing a nearby escape route, if needed. She silently stands before the garden bed, head bowed in non-recognition of this man's menacing presence.

Huxley speaks, "Bethany, you seem to be a bit uncomfortable around me. Why is that? I mean you no harm…don't you remember our little conversation the day I stopped by your school to visit with you?" Bethany musters a weak, "I remember…"

"Well, then…" Huxley continues, "how about we continue our little chat now?" Bethany, raises her eyes to meet his and defiantly whispers, "But I don't want to!" She then pivots her body and begins to head back to the security of her home, only to be stopped by a firm grip about her tiny arm, the pressure ever increasing as Huxley bends down and whispers in her ear, sending an ice-cold chill down her spine... "But I insist!"

Without warning Bethany's tiny frame whips around and faces Bryon Huxley dead on and begins... "You are not welcome here! You need to leave!", the voice emanates from Bethany's mouth, but it is not Bethany who is speaking...it is the voice of The Keeper!

While startled by the command coming from Bethany's form, Byron Huxley soon realizes that it is not she who is speaking these words and finds himself immobilized to the spot in which he stands; or, more truthfully, a captive to an unseen force until his release is unilaterally executed. All the while, the rest of the family goes about their business, completely unaware of what is transpiring just a few short yards away in the garden.

Bethany remains before Huxley, mouth agape as the words from The Keeper resume:

We have allowed this moment of discourse but not for the reasons you may be wanting. We are well aware of your presence and of your...um...agenda concerning The Program.

We are also knowing that your requisite to survive and regenerate on this Earth experience is in severe jeopardy due to your vehicle's accelerated deterioration. You seek our science in such matters and covet we will be of assistance in your quest to overcome this physical destruction...but that will not be! Not now...not in the future!

We are here to declare that your existence is coming to closure and that further efforts to engage with this vehicle known as Bethany will be met with disagreeable means to your remaining physicality.

I, am The Keeper! I am charged with the safeguard of this young human and compelled to see that she remains unharmed by any earthbound entities, stellar or interdimensional, for her mission is paramount to future exchanges from multi-galactic races.

Your efforts will remain unsatisfied and futile. Go now! You are no longer bound to this time and space. Prepare whatever soul you may possess for its ultimate climax for the time has come for its extinction and transition. I am complete!

As Byron Huxley struggles to remain erect from the unexpected and powerful encounter with The Keeper, Bethany is drawn back from her suspended trance state, unaware of The Keeper's interception on her behalf. All she knows is that Mr. Huxley is stumbling his way back to the house without speaking. For whatever reason, Bethany no longer feels threatened by this man and, in fact, feels pity for him, for her intuition allows her to view his time left on earth is fleeting.

Once back inside the house, Huxley declares to his hosts that he has fallen ill, which Larry silently notes by his guest's apparent deteriorated demeanor and offers to take him back to his hotel, which he agrees to unwaveringly. Nothing more needs to be said…this evening's visit has come to an abrupt end, with no chance of reoccurrence in the future.

A barely there smile slowly emits from Bethany's lips as she watches Huxley's departure, intuitively confidant she's seen the last of him.

MILABS

Without warning or precognition, my life had taken an unexpected turn - more like a spiral! My abilities that I once viewed as somewhat playful and well...kinda cool, were now the cause of much concern and an added element of danger began to loom quite large.

The sleep study I had done with Liz, while ground breaking for the scientific community, opened a Pandora's Box in a world I wasn't even aware existed, the underworld of the Secret Government also referred to as the Black Op. The best way to explain the Black op is that it is a clandestine operation by a government, or government agency, and can sometimes also be part of a military organization. Their main objective is to provide a significant degree of deception in an effort to conceal who is really behind their agenda or, better yet, to deflect activities to another entity.

One such organization was known as MILABS. MILABs is an acronym that refers to "military abductions." Military personnel are seen, sometimes working alone, but more likely working alongside alien beings.

Current thinking surrounding these activities suggests they are actually aliens, or alien-human hybrids dressed in military uniforms. They are thought to be a highly secretive group of specially trained humans using alien technology who are working with one or more groups of aliens. While others claim this is all an illusion perpetrated by "mind control" agents which are created via technology such as neural implants, holographs and wave technology. What this all boils down to is that these virtual *reality scenarios or VRS are real and pretty intimidating stuff, no matter the explanation.*

I learned about the MILAB program the hard way but didn't actually know anything more concrete about them until I was almost an adult.

At any rate, their agenda is to learn everything they can about the alien's motives and activities so, it wasn't all that surprising that they would want to talk with me. But I found out... that they didn't just want to talk....

(Flashback)

Bethany's nightly sojourns to the play house usually begin after she has fallen into a deep sleep. She has grown accustomed to feeling the intense vibrational hum that permeates every fiber of her being, accompanied by a dizzying closed eye swirl of colors that signal her inter-dimensional journey to join her hybrid friends has begun...again.

Not able to control any portion of her unearthly transport, Bethany can only observe and receive the sensations and sounds that are part of the process. Only this time...something is different. *Very different.*

The vibrational tones which are normally pleasant, have become brash and ear piercing. The customary vibrant colors have muddied and are bleak. Bethany struggles in her conscious mind to interpret what is happening but cannot. This whole process is totally unfamiliar to her and she begins to feel a sense of panic arise from deep within.

About the time Bethany is about to scream aloud, she is jolted back to full consciousness...but her arrived destination is beyond her comprehension.

Her surroundings are unwelcoming and sterile. As she labors to identify her setting, she whispers aloud, "This can't be the play house...and if it is...why is it so scary and where are the others? Where is The Keeper? Where is Daphne?"

Within seconds, it is made abundantly clear that she is NOT in the play house!

Then, a presence comes in to focus. It is a pale-skinned, stern looking woman who takes a dazed and confused Bethany firmly by the hand and all but drags her down a long, winding, lifeless hallway. The only illumination is that of an occasional lantern type lighting that casts ominous shadows at every turn.

Bethany is frightened beyond words, and while she has grown accustomed to her unconventional transport to the play house, she recognizes how this is not the same.

Bethany's vocal protests and any other attempts to resist or challenge her captor as to where they are going are met with harsh verbal admonishment, coupled with an even firmer grip about her petite wrist; if that was at all possible, for the grip is so taught that Bethany can feel her blood pulsating at the tips of her fingers.

When at last they appear to reach their destination, the unobtrusive wall before them opens in complete silence, revealing a stark, cold, circular room, with an oblong, silver metallic table draped in white material with several imposing machines at one end. There is a large, oversized light that hangs low to the table. Bethany can't help but compare this light to those found in a dentist's treatment room, only this one is so much larger.

On either side of the table stands four figures, all dressed in long, white, one-piece pant coverings; their heads bear white caps with what appears to be some type of headband with a small, round, metal object. To Bethany, it resembles a single car headlight, not yet illuminated. Surgically gloved hands hang loosely at their sides. All but their eyes are covered in surgical masks, and yet Bethany is sure that three of the four are male and one is female.

As Bethany continues her involuntary walk inside this foreboding chamber, she notes others are present...hidden slightly in the shadows. Her eyes dart first in one direction, then in another as she attempts to consider what is about to happen next.

Once reaching the table side, she is immediately hoisted onto its top by the woman who led her into this foreboding room. The others standing off to the side, step in, and without haste, swiftly immobilize Bethany by placing two large, black, leather straps about her tiny frame; one that is secured tightly about her chest, confining her arms and hands and; the second strap is placed over her knee area, prohibiting any leg movement.

Before she can let out the primal scream that awaits from within, a voice only heard by her, within her head, instructs, "Just lay back Bethany. It will be over soon...All will be well."

The voice is familiar to her, so she seeks out its source. Eyes straining under the harsh light just above her tiny body, she squints in desperation to make out the figures along the wall, but all she can make out are military type uniforms, with caps that hide the majority of their owner's face.

Then she spots him. The tall figure with oversized head and almond shaped eyes...The Keeper? The Keeper is here?

"Help me! You've got to help me? What are they doing? Why am I here?

H-E-L-P ME-E-E!!! Bethany finally shouts at the top of her lungs believing that he'll make everything alright again, for she has come to trust him and his stewardship of her well-being.

The occupants in the room know full-well to whom this plea is directed and turn their heads in unison in obvious warning to him to remain where he is, to which he complies.

The decades long-held partnership between the United States government and certain alien cultures to allow medical and psychological experimentation of humans in exchange for the alien's advanced technologies, has mandated certain rules of conduct that can never be questioned nor disobeyed. NEVER!

It is understood and acknowledged that the race of beings the government has been working with do not demonstrate emotion of any kind and abide by these conventions since their agenda is strictly one of science. They simply do not possess the ability to feel emotion. It's not part of their DNA.

"Gentlemen, please begin", a monotoned male voice from the shadows instructs.

All at once, the room comes to life as the four white clothed bodies go about their assigned duties; one reaches over Bethany's head to lower the piercing white light even closer, while another clicks the toggle switches of the equipment that sits behind her small head to the "on" position.

Bethany's heart is racing so fast and pumping so hard she is positive it will burst out of her chest at any moment. Words are no longer possible, as fear has dried the saliva in her mouth, leaving her helpless to emit any further pleas. But in her head, her desperate screams for help continue to the only one that can hear them.

The woman of the group holds in her hand a head cap of wires and probes that she is about to place on Bethany's skull, not unlike the apparatus she donned during her sleep study with Liz and yet, she is utterly frozen with fear. From the soft mumblings by the observers, Bethany can barely make out their words, "How much pain will this cause her?... and how much permanent impairment will it do to her brain?"

Bethany fully comprehends the asker's questions and so moves into full-on panic and hysterics, twisting and jerking her young body about as much as is humanly possible, despite the leather restraints. What should be a most disturbing sight to witness is met with an emotionless directive by one of the onlookers to prepare a sedative, which is to be administered immediately!

Another voice cautions that, in his opinion, the implementation of any drug would not only hinder the procedure and its goal but prove to be a worthless exercise. The medical debate continues for but a moment until a shrill voice commands, "Just put on the God damn device, NOW!"

So, this was it…this was the point of no return.

In an eon of a second, Bethany determines her ultimate fate and stares blankly beyond the harsh light to the ceiling, mentally commanding her spirit to leave her body that would soon be rendered not as she was before.

Her thoughts swiftly move to the members of her beloved family, Mom, Dad, Charlie and Ryan and how she will truly miss them. Just before closing her eyes to receive her doom, disruptive sounds explode Bethany back into her body forcing her to refocus on the happenings in the room.

To her shock, looming before her stands The Keeper; and without effort, easily rips the leather constraints away from her body and lifts her carefully into his awaiting spindly arms. Any attempts to interfere with his mission are met fiercely by piercing, telepathic sound waves which he emits from his being, driving the room's occupants to their knees. Defensively, they hold their hands over their ears, writhing in pain, leaving them no choice but to back off. Ironically, Bethany feels no pain from this emission, as The Keeper surrounds her in an invisible protective cocoon just prior to commencing his astonishing action.

With Bethany now safely in his control, The Keeper walks committedly to the locked door, glances over to the keypad that holds the combination of their retreat and with one blinding, laser flash from his normally darkened eyes, frees the pair from the bounds of the room.

The remainder of their retreat is uneventful, as The Keeper strategically ensures that they are now undetectable as he crosses them both over into an unseen dimension of safety.

UNLIKELY HERO

*O*ne thing I learned right away when interacting with the hybrids in my travels to the play house, was that the being I referred to as "The Keeper", was in charge. However, there were other, tall, somewhat ominous figures that stood apathetic and un-reactive to whatever was happening in their presence; with the exception of an occasional crying human child, who would immediately be taken by the hand and led out of the play house area by one of the other "Keepers." No coddling, no words of comfort, no questions asked about why they were crying, just removal from the room. When and if they returned, it was only because the human child was no longer upset and could resume the "lessons" without incident. End of story.

These beings were void of any emotion or any expression for that matter, and stood passively against the walls during our visits, only intervening with the kids and the hybrids when absolutely necessary.

However, The Keeper at my area, was different somehow. At least that's how I perceived him. Right from the start, he and I had a connection, a relatability that surpassed an otherwise inanimate, android demeanor that kept a dispassionate watch.

In all honesty, and I say this with unabashed pride, that I was infinitely bolder than most of the other human children, charged with my astonishingly eager curiosity and determination to get answers. And so, during my telepathic communications with The Keeper, I would occasionally look deeply into the dark abyss of his eyes, challenging him to break character. Every once in a while, I swore I detected a glimmer of light, a spark of feeling... but it would disappear in a heartbeat, as soon as I made mental *note of it; I was sure he was deliberately blocking entrance into his soul, if he had one. Wasn't sure about that either...until...*

(Flashback)

The Keeper walks with commitment as he holds Bethany steadfast in his cold, spindly rubber-like arms. Having rescued her from the MILAB chamber from what could have been a torturous experimentation by the surreptitious medical team, The Keeper utilizes his aptitude to transport both he and his precious cargo through a dimensional veil; a process that still alludes the brightest of the bright in the scientific communities around the planet. It is one of the withholds that the aliens refuse to give up to their human counterparts in this strange partnership of experimentation and technological exchange.

Bethany lies silent in The Keeper's embrace, emotionally and physically spent from the trauma that has befallen her. She has no thoughts, no visions, no impressions, just exhaustion and is completely reliant on The Keeper's momentum, removing them out of harm's way.

When their final destination is reached, The Keeper slowly lowers Bethany's small frame upon a soft and inviting surface that she perceives is like a bed, of sorts. Her weary eyes struggle to make out any other items in this space. Doesn't matter. She can't think about anything else right now. Just needs sleep. She needs to escape into a zone of silence, a safe haven where the horrors of the day melt into fragmented memories that will dissipate in slumber. Before drifting off into a deep state of nothingness, she releases a soft, distressing whimper... *"Mommy..."*

THE KEEPER SPEAKS

After being rescued by The Keeper from undisputable life-threatening harm by my unknown abductors, I knew, beyond a doubt that my life as I had known it was forever changed and that my childhood innocence, with all its uncharacteristic happenings, had taken a sinister turn into the darkest depths of the shadow world, that even I couldn't have foreseen.

And that's something that most people don't understand...while I have this amazing...um...er...talent for seeing events that are about to happen to others, this skill isn't always accessible when it comes to my own life.

Oh, don't get me wrong, when something was about to happen to me, I would get that "gut" feeling; but whenever I attempted to tune in to the energy and "read" what it was about, it just didn't happen. So, I learned that my gift was meant for others and that I was just like everyone else when it came to the unknown of my future. Frustrating, for sure...but it was, what it was.

By the same token, when it came to my visits with The Keeper, I intuitively trusted him...which proved to be sound, especially given his heroic feat of saving me from those that would have done me harm, if not killed me...all in the name of advancing science, yet more unquestionably, their covert agenda.

But what he did following that rescue was unfathomable and something I didn't fully grasp or appreciate at the time. Had I been wrong and naïve in putting so much faith in his protection of me without knowing what HIS own agenda was? I was about to find out.

(Flashback)

As Bethany awakes from her respite from the terrifying events in the MILAB, she fights to release the emotional coma of yesterday's trauma. Sitting upright, she rubs her eyes in an attempt to awake more fully and is surprised to find she's not back in the comfort and safety of her own bedroom, which is what normally happens after one of her nightly sojourns.

Her surroundings, while unfamiliar, are pleasant. The small bed is overlaid with a soft-hued quilted comforter; the walls are coated in a calming green and while there are no windows, colorful galactic images of the heavens and planets far beyond her world encircle this temporary sanctuary. To her amazement, lying next to her on the pillow is her beloved stuff animal Fred, just like he would be found at home, but she's not home.

Bethany desperately seeks to grasp where she is and why she's not been returned to her own dimension. As has been her custom in times of distress, she begins to sing in a low whisper…*Row, Row, row your boat, gently down the stream…merrily, merrily, merrily, merrily… life is but…*

This time, the singing fails to reassure Bethany, but just before panic launches into an epic proportion, a familiar figure appears…The Keeper!

Stealthily, he approaches her bedside and initiates a telepathic conversation:

The Keeper: *Bethany, you are well rested?*

Bethany: *I'm Okay…but, where am I? Why aren't I home? And how did Fred get here?*

The Keeper: *To answer the last query, I thought …um…Fred would bring you comfort. Was that incorrect? And as to where are you…the best way for me to articulate that is to say...you are safe here. No one can harm you in this place behind the veil. Does that please you?*

The very fact that The Keeper asked if she was "pleased" surprised Bethany, for he was not known to possess emotions of any kind, let alone compassion.

The conversation continues:

The Keeper: *You have experienced much and consequently, in that I am charged with your well – being, I performed a mind amalgamation ...um... you would call it... "read your mind" and found things that would be pleasing to you and provide calm to your organism. These things that you see are but holograms of things in your world... not physical...let me rephrase...real.*

The Keeper pauses for a moment, tilts his head as if contemplating his next words, then resumes:

The Keeper: *I know not why I engage in such action on your behalf, as it is not comportment of my race to provide such concern. It is foreign to me, nonetheless, I was compelled to do so. Again, do these things bring you calm and preference?*

Bethany: *Ya, but...I...I...um... wanna go home! I'm scared and I d-d-don't want those p-p-people to find me again. Will they find me. again?*

Bethany's eyes fill to the brim with tears, that race uncontrollably down her flushed checks.

The Keeper: *It is in the realm of possibilities that they will seek you out again, as they feel you have much to share with them about your interaction with the ...um...others...our spawn...the hybrids... predominantly...Daphne. Does that offer clarity?*

Bethany: *But w-what do they want? I don't know what I could tell them...I'm just there to play. Why do they want to h-hurt me?* (Bethany buries her face into her trembling hands, breathing heavily through her pitiful sobs.)

The Keeper: *Bethany, I have much to tell you, so I would ask that you listen well. You may ask me questions when I am finished ...but for now...you must absorb fully the words that I am to speak. Do you understand?*

Bethany lifts her tear-stained face to look directly into The Keepers eyes; those duel black chasms searching for resolution - reaches for Fred, cradling him tightly to her chest, then nods in agreement.

The Keeper: *I will attempt to speak in a way that things are clear for you to understand. I have altered your brainwaves in such a way that you will follow even the most difficult terminologies for a human of your age, so that I may speak what you must hear.*

 Let me proceed...

 The beings from my planet have interacted with the organisms of Earth for millennium. Some interactions have been peaceful, while others have of a more negative energy.

 There are those in your government who have made a partnership with our planet...that is, collectively it has been agreed that in exchange of our advanced technologies we will be given access to certain humans for scientific evaluation and experimentation.

 One such experimentation called for the interaction of human children who displayed exceptional abilities relative to telepathic communication and interdimensional transportation. You were one of those children...You were chosen to be part of this Program. You come from a human lineage that has these special aspects; your father being one, your full-biological brother, Ryan, the other. Your mother does not have these abilities, nor does your half-biological brother Charles. It is your full paternal bloodline that allows these abilities to be passed down from generation to generation. The choice of each human to utilize these abilities is individual. We cannot interfere with the process of acceptance or rejection.

Your father helped us in the past, but then disallowed his participation for reasons unknown to us, so his remembering was deleted and he was immediately eliminated from the Program. He knows of your "gifts", as you express in Earth terms but chose not to encourage them. He will soon learn of Ryan's exceptionality but is not yet recognized.

The ones you refer to as Liz, Stephan and Daphne... (I believe she chooses to be known as Krystal now,) have also been chosen to be part of the Program but are not of your planet. As hybrids, they're interaction with you is paramount and will continue at another time. For now, that's all you need to know.

It has been unfortunate that there are humans of a less positive energy who want only to control the masses and keep the knowledge we share, to themselves. They are greedy and have an agenda that is of suspect to the good of all.

While my planet's inhabitants have been viewed as hostile by earthlings, it is of great irony that it is the earthlings, who possess such characteristics and are, in fact, of great concern throughout the galaxy that we share and beyond.

For now, what I need you to know and understand is this... your interaction with the hybrids has been vital in helping different galactic species understand one another. In that understanding, since we are the ones who possess the ability to traverse between dimensions and technologically achieved intergalactic travel between planets, we came to you... rather than you to us. So that we may walk among you undetected, it had become necessary to *utilize one of your planet's greatest resources for the education we sought...your children.*

Children are born into your human experience unfiltered and open to all possibilities. It is only through fear and control that the abilities that humans are born with, while inferior to our young, are discouraged and not nurtured.

By the Earth age of five, most children lose their natural intuitive aptitude and telepathic communication skills, as the human parents enforce the use of verbal language onto their offspring. Unfortunate misjudgment to take away the traits that come naturally and are of benefit to all.

This is a practice that has mistakenly been passed down from generation to generation and it is only those who cannot deny or contradict these abilities who rise above the rest.

It is a curiosity that humans would want to eliminate these abilities and choose to "dummy themselves down" ... I believe that is the Earth term I seek... to be like all the others and not excel in what comes natural to them.

You are one who cannot readily dismiss that what comes natural to you...but hear this...so that you may be harmless and continue with the Program...I have been charged with disconnecting your state of knowledge, until such time it is safe for you to resume.

What I mean by this is...I will close down your abilities, erase all memories of what has been, so that those who would do you harm will see that you no longer possess what they want. This is being done for your continuance, as they would end up destroying your vehicle...um...body.

We wish to have you continue with the Program, as you have much to share and can be of great significance to both species.

Know this...you will be reinstated and your memory will return when, and only when it has been determined wise to do

*so. You will be rendered "normal", "just like the other kids",
by all. For those who have knowledge of your abilities and are
determined to make negative use of them, they will be deliberately
misinformed into believing you no longer possess these faculties.*

*One more thing...you will not have any memory of me, or of
our interactions. When the time is right, you will begin receiving
momentary retentions, I believe they are called "flashbacks."
These will serve as a reintroduction to what has been before
so that you may move more fully into the next phase of your
teachings.*

Now, if you have the need...I will hear your questions...

Again, Bethany eyes fill with tears as she begins to understand, at
least, part of what The Keeper has told her. Her mind races with
a flurry of questions... and so begins:

Bethany: *I...um...uh...think I understand what you're
telling me, ...um... BUT what's going to happen
to me when you take away the things that I can
do? I mean...um...how I know things...um...
what about my talking in my head to Ryan or
Daphne...um...er...or YOU! If that's all gone...
then what will I be like?*

The Keeper tilts his head as he ponders the best explanation for
his young charge and answers:

The Keeper: *Bethany, your ability to 'talk in your head' or
know things that are about to unfold for others, is
but a skill that you were born with. It is, however,
NOT who you are...it is merely what you can do.*

*Consider this... some humans come into their
physical experience able to understand music at
its purest form. They have no need for lessons or
teachings...they merely understand the complexity
of that skill without being shown by another. So, it
has been with you that your capability to see, hear*

and feel what others cannot, simply provides you with a knowing about that which eludes others. But again, I insist that you distinguish your talents from who you are...as they are not one in the same.

Bethany struggles to agree with The Keeper's explanation.

Bethany: *Ya but...I'm used to knowing stuff and talking in my head...I'll miss that...won't I?*

The Keeper: *You will not remember that you have those abilities, even though some may attempt to remind you of them. You will simply BE who you are. If I may continue:*

You will also discontinue your human learning at the space for others such as yourself and retreat to a place of lesser knowledge. There will, however, be one from that higher space of learning who will continue in your journey. I believe he is called Jarred. His role with you will be uncovered at a future time and place.

I must direct you to one other change that may be most difficult...your connection with the one known as Krystal, I believe you refer to as Daphne, whom you met in the play house, will be just another child to you. You may even reject her attempts to continue your connection; you will view her only as an oddity, a child that you don't wish to know.

This is necessary due to those who wish to do you grave harm because of your interaction with off planet beings such as she, so it is paramount for your physical continuance to disconnect any correlation with her and the others of her origin, thus proving that you no longer possess what they seek. It must be. There is no other way.

Bethany: *Will I be laughed at...made fun of or will I be... just like the other kids? I mean...it would be nice...um...I guess...to not be teased or made fun of or feel different...I guess...*

Bethany is coming to terms with what will be, but has yet to grasp fully the fact that by temporarily erasing her memory will not only protect her from the government's MILAB abductions but prohibit others, such as Byron Huxley from exploiting her for their own despicable agendas.

Bethany: *When will this happen?*

The Keeper: *It has already begun...*

Bethany: (sighs)...*I wanna go home now...*

JARRED

*A*s an adult, now looking back along what I like to refer to as my physical trail, I've had some pretty amazing things happen, some more petrifying and remarkable than others and yet, all in all, a most unique life I'd say.

But more than the experiences themselves, I've been surrounded by a community, of sorts, one that sought only to support, nurture and (the biggest thing of all) protect me. Oh, of course I expected that my parents would be my prime barrier and safeguard but still, at times, I wondered if that were enough.

When I was enrolled in the school for gifted kids, (something I had been made to temporarily forget) there were lots of adults around us, always watching, evaluating and desperately trying to figure out who we were and how they could best cope with our not-so-easy temperaments. You can only imagine what our poor teachers had to deal with on any given day, given the level of high-strung energy that simply could not be contained. So, instead they chose to simply 'ride herd' over the brood of unpredictability and hope the hands on the clock would move faster, heralding the end of the school day.

I'll bet dollars to donuts that more than one educator lifted a glass or two at the end of the day in hopes of diminishing their chaotic memories. Can you blame them?

As far as the kids, themselves, well, as you can imagine, there was a lot of competition, a one-upmanship as to who possessed the most unique abilities and often challenged one another on the playground exhibiting their individual areas of expertise.

The challenges would be more in the realm of...who could read whose mind...or who could show off their skills in kinetics by manipulating a twig from a fallen branch to rise from the *ground, or spiral a rock a few feet across the playground's concrete. Silly, I know, but what else did you expect these kids to do during recess...swing on swings or hop on to the teeter-totter? Well, actually...some of us did...(chuckling).*

The age range for the kids at this school varied greatly. And even though I was in the youngest age group, some of the kids in my special...um...a...let's say...area of proficiency, were so advanced from the others, that the older kids simply steered clear of us. What's that saying? Don't judge a book by its cover...well, don't judge a kid by his/her age or size. That's just genetics.

The funny thing was, those kids who truly had the most... um...powers, if you will, never used them to harm or intimidate the others...even when teased or bullied to 'show me what you got!' Those challenges were met with exceptional maturity and calm, proving, to me at least, that they knew how powerful they were so there was no need to show off to any extreme degree, especially knowing that someone could get hurt...and it wouldn't be the kids that were being bullied, if you get my drift.

One day, a malevolent man, came by the school and watched all of us playing during recess from his huge, ominous looking, black car. I picked up on his energy right away and while I felt he was up to no good as I watched him exit the vehicle and approach the chain linked fence surrounding the playground, I was compelled to walk towards him, almost trance like, yet extremely cavalier about any possible danger. Can't tell you why, but I did.

This man identified himself as Byron Huxley (the same man who later on had been invited into our home under the guise as a "client" of my father's CPA firm) and told me that he knew of my special...skills...and desperately needed my help connecting with the hybrids. Well, it didn't take long for me to realize that I had overstepped my normally good judgment and had perhaps placed myself in jeopardy, but that's when I discovered that my protection not only came from the intervention of the school chaperons, along with The Keeper, but unbeknownst to me at the time, a third unexpected protector was at hand - an older classmate named Jarred.

I knew nothing of Jarred's protection of that day, nor did I consider, even remotely, the role Jarred would have in my journey...until many years later.

(Flashback)

After The Keeper artfully disengaged Bethany's capacities, her life became uneventful. Her mother Rachel was thrilled that her daughter finally acted like a normal kid and so saw no more need for Bethany to attend the school for "gifted kids." All Rachel knew or cared about was that her child was finally "cured" of whatever THAT was and could now live a regular life with none of the nonsense that had gone before.

Ryan, would often question his sister about why she didn't talk about her night time visits to the play house or her little friends with the funny heads and big black eyes anymore. Not remembering any of it, Bethany simply chalks it up to Ryan's wild imagination and cajoles him off subject. Doesn't take Ryan long to stop asking and accepts his big sister's teasing, and yet longs for the resumption of their telepathic communications, which are no longer happening.

Whenever Ryan attempts to "talk" to Bethany as they have done all their young lives, he is met with silence. It is as if the energy line of communication had been cut off completely... which, in fact...it had.

Bethany resumes her education at a local public school. She is well liked and has no memory of the school she once attended, her special classmates or Daphne. It was as if it all never happened. With one exception, Jarred.

Not knowing how or why Bethany's memory has been altered, Jarred astutely assumes a "higher power" has intervened for the sake of her well-being. For he is wise beyond his years and savvy to the caution that must be taken when dealing with the seen and unseen dark forces that abound and stalk these special children. So, he deliberately chooses to circumvent any details or specific references of Bethany's time at the school and lets it be enough that she has a passing memory of being at another school for a short time, but more importantly, of him.

The years pass quickly by and now it is time for her high school graduation. As long as Bethany can remember, Jarred has always been a part of her social group. It didn't hurt one bit that Jarred had turned into a bit of a hottie and was very easy to be around, both for his good looks and his charming personality. It never mattered to her that he went to a special school for super smart kids, for he chose to engage his social time with the "regular kids." She liked that about him.

Every once in a while, Jarred went against his better judgement and attempted to jar Bethany's memory, but was left frustrated, as those memories simply didn't exist for her any longer. He doesn't fight her on it, as all he cares about is being around her. For whatever reason, Bethany feels the same.

After graduating with extreme high honors from his school, Jarred was offered a job working as an advanced digital instrumentation technologies specialist nationwide and was presented with the unique opportunity to train an exclusive staff of engineers at NASA's Space Center. Pretty impressive.

One of his favorite travels took him to Arizona State University. As luck would have it, his aunt and uncle on his mother's side lived in Scottsdale, so he stayed with them every chance he got when traveling to the Southwest.

On one of his visits, his uncle encouraged him to take a drive up to Sedona, a two hour, one-hundred-twenty-mile trek north of the Phoenix Metro Valley. At an altitude of approximately four thousand-five hundred feet, this was no ordinary high-desert environment – quite the opposite. Jarred had fallen in love with the area and swore, one way or the other, that he'd get Bethany to fly out West to join him for some hiking and exploration of this magical place with its Red Rock monoliths and the numerous energy vortex centers– it was that important to him.

So, at Jarred's enthusiastic prompting, he convinces Bethany's parents to purchase a plane ticket as her graduation gift, destination – Phoenix Arizona's Sky Harbor Airport and a once in a lifetime vacation to the majesty of Sedona. He assures them that Bethany is more than welcome to stay with his aunt and uncle in nearby Scottsdale, so all she needs is some "mad money." It was such a wonderful opportunity and the perfect gift for their amazing daughter who has just graduated high school with her own high honors. Done!

As the time grows closer for her trip to the Southwest, Bethany begins to experience some strange feelings, rumblings of "something" that tugs deep within; not identifiable as out and out anxiety, yet just short of over enthusiasm to seeing her long-time friend, Jarred. Unable to get a handle on the whys, Bethany chooses to dismiss these feelings as over excitement, not only to visit a new place but to have an opportunity to be with Jarred again, for it has been way too long since they'd seen one another.

Oh, they kept in touch and talked for hours on the phone, albeit a bit tricky with the three-hour time difference. More often than not, Bethany would burn the midnight oil waiting for Jarred's call when his day was done at his job and would find herself stumbling through the next day's activities blurry eyed and not firing on all cylinders, but to her…it was all worth it.

Bethany isn't exactly clear on what her feelings for Jarred are, can't label them as yet, but he certainly has an impact on her and she knows without a doubt that he is destined to be in her life for a long time to come, in whatever role is to be. Her sleeping intuition aside, she feels that on such a deep level.

At long last the day has arrived and Bethany unmercifully hurries her parents out the door and into the family car finally heading for the airport.

With older brother, Charlie now living in Chicago working as a junior ad executive for a sports clothing firm, while younger brother Ryan is off at a friend's house, supposedly studying for his final exams before entering his junior year in high school, Bethany has her loving parents all to herself. She prattles on about what she and Jarred have planned to do once she arrives. In fact, he's created a pretty hectic schedule for the two young explorers, what with hikes among the Red Rock terrain, a trip to the Grand Canyon and lots of sightseeing in nearby Jerome, an old mining ghost town, a drive through the switchbacks to Flagstaff and even a few night time excursions to look for U.F.O.'s, Sedona's claim to fame for the plethora of paranormal activity. Exciting stuff for sure.

Once her bag is checked in at the airline counter, Bethany bids her family a hasty *"See ya soon!"* and all but skips her way to her departure gate, excited about seeing Jarred and what adventures await.

REUNION

*J*arred was right! I, too, fell in love with Sedona! Never, ever
had a place impacted me in such an intense way as Sedona
had...on this planet at anyway. (smiling)

*At the risk of sounding somewhat cliché, this amazing high
desert climate simply blew me away!*

*While Jarred incessantly talked my ear off about how much I
was going to love Sedona, he was careful not to tell me too much
about it, as he wanted me to experience it purely from my own
perspective. And I'm here to tell you....it did not disappoint!*

*I was in awe of its towering Red Rock monoliths, some that
were pointed out to me as resembling either cartoon characters
such as Snoopy and Lucy from "Peanuts" fame, to structures
aptly named Cathedral Rock or Bell Rock due to their obvious
configurations.*

*I was mesmerized by the influence of the energy vortexes and
a palpable spirituality that permeated every inch of the nineteen
plus miles of this mystical dessert topography. The rich landscape
was complimented by lush, green Ponderosa Pine, a variety of
blossoming cacti and the sweet fragrances of Rosemary and Sage
that filled the air.*

*I took full advantage of the hiking trails through the numerous
spiritual vortexes which were hailed for their powerful and
transformational energy centers. I learned that these vortexes
are caused by the intersection of natural electromagnetic earth
energies; in layman's terms, they are known as ley lines. These
energy centers not only affect the human body but also impact
Mother Nature's landscaping, as evidenced by the many twisted*

trees which were contorted not just by wind and weather, indicating the presence of this unseen force.

For the longest time, Jarred had wanted me to experience this unique place with him and for that I am most grateful for the introduction. But there was more... a "calling" of sorts... an overpowering pull to return, and so I took every opportunity to schedule even a long weekend, when I could afford it, to this magical Mecca. Something inside of me was burgeoning to surface whenever I traveled there; a compulsion that I simply couldn't ignore and needed to explore further...by myself. And so, I did...

(Flashback)

After her arrival at Phoenix Sky Harbor Airport, Bethany stands in front of the car rental counter finishing up the paperwork before heading "up the hill", some one hundred - twenty miles from the floor of Metro-Phoenix area to the vastly different terrain of the high desert country and Sedona, Arizona.

Having traveled to Sedona many times before with her good friend, Jarred, Bethany has a little trepidation of making this sojourn solo. Jarred has business obligations that prohibit his tagging along but makes her promise to share all the details of her visit. While Bethany always enjoys her time with Jarred, this time she has another agenda, one that she must pursue by herself.

Unable to explain even to herself why this is such a necessary excursion, she robotically carries out the mundane tasks in preparation of the two-hour road trip.

With keys in hand, Bethany takes the airport shuttle to the parking lot where her silvery blue Ford Focus awaits. Bethany is pleased with her assigned transportation but hopes it has enough oomph to handle the gradual incline challenges Interstate I-17 provides to all vehicles. Full peddle to the metal, still only renders an optimum speed of around forty-five miles per hour until the highway levels off enough to resume a high rate of speed.

The drive goes by without incident and in no time at all, Bethany delights when the large green and white sign that reads "SEDONA" comes into view. Turning off I-17, she begins to see evidence of the famed red clay earth that heralds the entrance into the Sedona area.

It never gets old for Bethany. The magnificent winding fourteen-mile winding route to Highway 89A; passing the famous Bell Rock formation located in the Village of Oak Creek, past the Chapel of the Holy Cross that is built right into the buttes. The magnificence of Cathedral Rock looms large on the opposite side of the two-lane road, with Courthouse Butte encompassing much of the view in the distance.

At last, Bethany reaches her destination, a modest motel that falls within her limited budget yet sits strategically central to all that she has come there to enjoy. After checking in, backpack in tow, Bethany takes a brief moment to ponder which one of the fabulous eateries she'll choose to quench her nagging hunger but already knows the answer...Javelina Cantina! Revered for having the most amazing authentic Mexican cuisine in the entire area, not to mention the panoramic view of the towering Red Rocks, makes this an easy choice.

After satiating her hunger and thirst, it isn't long before Bethany realizes that she'd be better served to simply go back to the motel to rest and lay out her plans for the next day's hike after her long travel day from the East Coast.

Bethany opens one of the smaller compartments of her backpack and dumps out its contents onto one of the twin beds in her unassuming motel room. While the numerous touristy brochures and pamphlets beckon for her attention, she's finding it hard to keep her eyes open and so pushes the pamphlets aside and gently settles her weary body down onto the bed and, in record time, falls fast asleep.

For the most part, Bethany's slumber is peaceful until sporadic flashes of random images cut into her dream state. The strobing visions have no relevant chronology, bouncing back and forth from pictures of her as a little girl with her brother Ryan, handing flowers to a neighbor, to sitting at a round table with other children, their appearance is anything but normal. Next, she observes two, very dark almond shaped eyes that send chills through her now fitful sleeping body, producing a deepening furrow upon her brow.

Unexpectedly, a loud bang from one of the other motel room doors in her corridor brings Bethany back to full consciousness, only to discover through her unclosed curtains that it is now totally dark outside. Her heart beats hard within her chest as she attempts to recount the disturbing images that infiltrated her catnap. Rubbing her eyes furiously, Bethany makes great effort to clear the cobwebs from the memories of her disturbing sleep.

The clock radio that sits atop the small nightstand between the twin beds reads "7:35 p.m." Wow! I slept a full five hours since lunch. Now what am I going to do? she wonders, still uneasy in the aftermath of her disquieting dreams...but where they just a dream?

Deep within Bethany knows something more has occurred but is unable to wrap her brain around what it all means and so decides to chock it up to travel fatigue and laughs it off.

With nothing else to do, she turns on the TV then channel surfs to a local Sedona station that advertises the areas featured activities and popular restaurants. Because she knows the area so well, she begins to refocus on her plans for the next day. Without much concentration, it is clear where she's headed...Cathedral Rock!

Not only is Cathedral Rock one of the most popular hikes for residents and visitors alike, Bethany feels that undeniable "tug" again when looking at the brochure's image of Cathedral Rock and says aloud… "Why fight the feeling… Cathedral Rock, here I come!"

The next morning arrives quickly, for which Bethany is most grateful, as she had worried about not being able to sleep after taking such a long and unexpected nap the day before. But that's Sedona for you. It's full of surprises and you have to be open to all possibilities.

There's a theory supported by the locals, that you must be careful what energy you bring into this unique environment, for it will come forth ten-fold. Any energy you possess is believed to be magnified by the electromagnetic field that surrounds the energy vortexes. Forewarned…is to be forearmed!

Bethany prepares her backpack for the day's hike; supplying it with plenty of bottled water, sunscreen, power energy bars and some fruit. But before she hits the trail, she heads down to the motel's lobby to partake of their modest Continental Breakfast. Must be mindful of my budget…

Once outside, Bethany lifts her head to the clear, crystal cobalt blue sky and closes her eyes, taking in a deep breath in gratitude for this glorious weather. Her heart is smiling.

After a short drive west on 89A, she points her car to Upper Red Rock Loop Road, a winding switchback with magnificent views of the lower regions. Within minutes she spies the sign "Red Rock Crossing – Cathedral Rock" which leads her to the gatehouse at the head of the parking area. Once the nominal entrance fee is paid, she directs her attention to a parking spot under one of several large trees that offer a welcome shade, as the high desert temperatures are touted to be up into the triple digits before her return trip.

With backpack strapped securely about her shoulders, sunscreen amply applied, Bethany captures her smooth long hair into a pony tail with an elastic type band, places a pale blue baseball cap upon her head and looks about the parking lot to determine where she wants her trek to begin.

The majority of the visitors are all going to the right portion of the park, obviously heading in the direction of the most photographed spot in the Crossing; a group of large red flat rocks which lies next to a crystal-clear river. But not Bethany, for she's compelled by other forces that usher her to go in the opposite direction, which she does without question or hesitation.

She follows a short cement path that leads to the entrance of a wooded area which boasts a small, natural pooled body of water. Bethany smiles to herself as she witnesses some older children jumping off the embankment rocks and squeal in amusement as they enter its chilly waters. Because Sedona is landlocked, young and old alike take full advantage of any opportunity to cool off from the hot desert sun wherever nature offers.

Continuing her walk through the arboreal path, she comes upon an open area that has several dozen tabletop red rocks which she effortlessly strolls across. At the far end of this rocked plaza, Bethany is met by the upper part of the water feature she just passed; more aptly described as a babbling book with its clear crystal water that rushes over river rocks and disembodied fallen tree branches.

Bethany observes a scattering of visitors here that have removed their shoes to dangle their feet in the coolness of this rapidly flowing body of water. Enticed Bethany finds her own spot, removes her sneakers and socks then ever so slowly dips her toes in first, letting out an uncontrollable shriek at how cold the water is. Didn't expect that...She chuckles to herself.

Determined to get past the initial shock of the frigid water, Bethany now cautiously lowers her feet into the water again, only this time is prepared for the jolt. One by one her toes submerge into the coolness until she lets out a sigh indicating that her body has accepted the glacial temperature and even finds it refreshing.

There is it again! Bethany feels that familiar "tug" to move on and so lifts her almost numb feet out of the brook's hold and puts her socks and sneakers back on, all the while glancing around to see where her exploration is to take her next.

Surprisingly, she chooses a thicketed forest, having to bob and weave her way through the growth until she comes upon an area that is like none other than she has ever seen, especially in the high desert terrain. There before her appears a large open area of multi-colored river rocks piled one on top of the other. Several of these rock towers loom quite large, while others only have four or five stones piled atop one another, almost defying gravity... fully balanced in their precarious placement.

What is this place? she wonders. She can't help but feel this is a place of reverence...for the architects' have taken great strides to construct these markers...no matter their meaning or purpose.

Intrigued, Bethany looks about and chooses several rocks of her own and carefully and stealthily manipulates her pieces to form a mini-monument of her own. Once steady and completed, Bethany stands back, takes stock of her creation and then lowers her head and closes her eyes as she emits a silent prayer of thanks. She has no idea why she did that...just felt that she should.

Feeling a renewed sense of peace and tranquility, Bethany moves on through the timbers to yet another small area that opens up to an unanticipated beach like setting, complete with dark beige sand and an inviting pool of water that reaches far across to the opposite embankment, complete with tire-rope swing. Amazing! she speaks aloud. Then giggles as she adds... "I'm NOT going in *THAT* water...it's probably just as cold as the last one!"

Bethany's stomach lets out an unflattering growl, indicating that now would be a great time to retrieve the goodies from her backpack and enjoy some lunch. She finds a flat rock down by the water's edge that resembles a rudimentary chair then slips her backpack off her shoulders, unzippers it to reveal the treasures that await within.

After taking a large gulp from the chilled water bottle, Bethany rips off the top part of the energy bar wrapper and begins enjoying the nutty, peanut butter and chocolate delight. Once fully consumed, Bethany removes a large red and yellow apple, takes a huge bite, then wipes away the juices that freely flow from the corners of her mouth.

Feeling satisfied from her mid-morning snack, Bethany reclines her body backward atop the rock, allowing the majority of her small frame to lay easily across its girth with only her legs dangling over onto the sandy shoreline. Using her backpack as a pillow, Bethany places her hands behind her head and stares at the fluffy white, billowing clouds that float high above across this astounding, vibrant sky, while the sun's rays gently rest upon her face.

Bethany lowers the visor of her baseball cap to shield the sun's beams and within moments is deep within a blissful repose without a thought in her head. Her lungs release a full-bodied sigh as she goes further and further into a peaceful slumber.

"Bethany... Bethany..." a voice softly calls...but she continues her respite.

"Bethany! BETHANY!" the voice is more urgent and is accompanied with a sensation that someone is standing beside where she lies.

Bethany bolts upright, wiping the sleep from her eyes, straining through the sunlight that bombards her face in an attempt to make out the figure that stands before her. Then she spots them... two amazingly brilliant, piercing blue eyes!

"Bethany...it's me...Daphne...er... I mean...Krystal! Don't you recognize me?"

Bethany struggles to full consciousness but more than that, she fights to recall the names that are being spoken, for she has no surface memory of the entity Daphne, now referred to as Krystal; or that they had briefly reconnected years ago at an outdoor eatery.

Bethany has no recollection that a large part of her childhood had been erased from her mind by The Keeper to forestall the dangers that lurked from those who wanted to do her harm because of her interaction with the hybrids.

Then, without warning, detailed flashbacks of her youth begin to explode; only this time through her conscious mind, not only in dream state. With each rebirth of memory, Bethany breathes hard and deep, like a marathon runner about to cross the finish line. Krystal watches intently and remains stoically by Bethany's side as she witnesses the unprecedented return of Bethany's remembrance through the eruptions of her memory's reactivation.

After what seems like an eternity, Bethany's breathing resumes to a more normal pace and the look of sheer panic diminishes from her previous confused gaze. Bethany slowly turns towards Krystal, as tears stream down her knowing eyes, for she remembers it all now and then calls out.... "Daphne? *KRYSTAL!*"

The two young friends fall into one another's embrace, allowing the moment its due justness.

THE AWAKENING –
KRYSTAL SPEAKS

*J*ust *prior to my first trip to Sedona after graduation from high school, I began experiencing weird dreams...well actually they were more than dreams...they were "rememberings", only I didn't see them as such at the time. But I have to tell you, some were beyond disturbing...terrifying was more like it!*

In some of these dreams, I was very young, as was my younger brother Ryan. I saw Ryan and I doing all manner of unusual things together; such as talking to one another in our heads, or what the other was thinking or feeling, at any given moment. Didn't matter whether we were in proximity of one another, or not.

Other images revealed me telling random people events and conversations that were about to happen to either them or their loved ones, like an impending death of a relative. Curious to me for sure, but again, I simply thought they were the product of my intense, albeit creative imagination. But it didn't stop there.

Most distressing were impressions of beings whose appearance ran just short of the macabre. I'm talking "Jurassic Park" reptilian forms that were covered in grey-green scales with red menacing eyes and yellow teeth that resembled a Tyrannosaurus Rex!

But the granddaddy nightmare of them all took place somewhere beneath the earth in dimly lit tunnels that were filled with the foul smell of something...well...dead.

I clearly remember walking in dream state through a subterranean, cavernous hallway and entering another area through a large metal doorway, whose only access was achieved by hitting a series of numerical codes on a keypad.

Once inside this new chamber, I stood frozen as my eyes scanned row after row of indescribable creatures housed in tall glass containers filled with a clouded amber liquid that perhaps was either life giving... or life preserving. Didn't matter...for all I knew was that I wanted to remove myself from this place and fast!

All of a sudden, I was abruptly being led by a woman I didn't know to another chamber and once inside I saw several military men and what appeared to be medical personnel standing around a metal table with lots of tubes and machinery. I instantly realized that I was the reason they were all there and that I was in extreme jeopardy and would suffer great bodily harm.

I screamed myself awake! I sat for hours shaking in my bed trying desperately to free my mind from recalling the vivid details of that nightmare.

I'd been having a recurring dream of a young woman with piercing blue eyes. Doesn't make sense, I know. Try as I might, I couldn't retain the dream long enough to provide me with a true recognition or reason why she kept appearing to me. I say "she" because that's what I interpreted the energy to be...feminine.

This much I knew...there was a reason she kept coming to me and one way or the other I was going to figure it all out. As for the other dreams...well, I chose to dismiss them and pivot my attention to more pleasant things.

With my solo trip to Sedona at hand, I did everything in my power to release those negative images and focus on the beauty and tranquility I knew I would experience once again among the magic of the Red Rock energy.

But what I was beginning to realize was now that Krystal and I had reconnected with one another, I was about to become fully awakened to those memories and experiences that had all been forgotten...or had been completely erased.

✦ (Flashback)

Bethany and Krystal stand in motionless silence, taking in this moment of reconnection and reunion on the sandy shore of Cathedral Rock's foothill basin.

Shaken to her very core, Bethany finally breaks the silence, "Man! I've got to sit down for a minute...the world is spinning... GOSH! Krystal? Krystal! ...

W-w-hat, w-why...*HOW* are you here? What does this mean? Help me out here!" Bethany spews in one long exhausting breath.

Krystal takes Bethany by both hands and helps to lower her back down upon the rock that she but moments ago sat upon before the revelation brought her abruptly to her feet.

Krystal knows that Bethany will have a million questions but asks to be indulged by holding those queries while she searches for fathomable language that will explain what has gone before and hopefully refreshes Bethany to full remembrance.

Krystal begins:

Bethany...I believe you are now able recall going to a place you refer to as the play house? (Bethany nods affirmatively) *and how we first came to be in one another's existence? Do you agree?* (again, an unspoken nod of confirmation from Bethany).

You and I have been brought forth...um...united in a common experiment...

Krystal struggles for the right words to relay what is of importance so that Bethany will grasp the whole picture.

Krystal continues:

Where I come from, our species is not all that different from Earth children, with a few exceptions of course, none more obvious than the differential in our physicality; and so, it was decided that an experiment would be most useful to determine if we could be taught the ways of human children so that we may blend in more easily when the time of integration arrived. By integration I mean, there are those throughout Earth's solar system, including my ancestors, who have been watching Earth and its inhabitants for some time and were aware of a cyclical astronomical event...sorry-rephrase...a returning planet that was due to be dangerously close to Earth by the year 2012, which is where we are now.

So, the Galactic Federation, a group of diverse benevolent Star Beings who oversee the vast cosmic space we share, concluded that if Earth's human civilization were to evolve and become part of the galactic neighborhood, due to their...how can I say this diplomatically?... insufficient knowledge of the workings of the Universe and lack of advanced technologies, an intervention was necessary. Whew! That was really difficult to put into Earth language, but I know you get what I'm trying to say.

Bethany is at full attention now, listening intently, trying to reach the place of complete understanding.

Krystal goes on:

Well, as it happens, I was one of the off-planet newbies who were selected, some of us in vitro, to assist in this experiment. Of course, it was a choice, not a mandate that we participate and so it followed that we would choose our Earth parents. Just how I did that is hard to explain but let it be enough to know that I could "experience" energy and after 'reviewing' the candidates, was inclined to choose two hybrids as my Earth mother and father. I'll explain all this in a minute and the role you played in that process.

Bethany is beyond intrigued and remains in full interest.

Krystal adds:

I'm about to celebrate the 12th marking of my emergence into physical...my birthday, but let me tell you, this celebration is anything BUT normal! Let me explain: I was born on December 21, 2000, the day of the Winter Solstice in the new Millennium. My birth was, how shall I say...um...extremely out of the ordinary, for my mother gave birth during a snow storm, here at the base of Cathedral Rock in ... in the water!

Bethany's eyes almost pop out of her head with this last declaration.

Krystal: *Okay, so now you're beginning to get the picture. I shall go on: A Hopi Indian spirit named Chumana, not only prophesized my birth but was present and aided in my emergence into physical form.*

Sadly, she also assisted in my mother's transition – for she died right after I came forth. I miss her very much. Okay, I can hear you ask, "How can you miss someone you never knew?" but you're wrong; I not only knew my mother before my birth but as I stipulated a few moments ago, but specifically chose her and my father to be my Earth parents, for they too, are hybrids.

While existing on this earth plane, my mom was a psychologist specializing in children who interacted with hybrids, who provided them with fundamental instruction on human characteristic behavior but were often mislabeled as abductees or contactees.

Beginning to connect the dots, Bethany shouts, "LIZ?"

Krystal: *Yes, I believe that is what you and others called her. As a hybrid herself, who better to understand these child emissaries whose parents and peers considered them majorly dysfunctional or just plain peculiar? She was brilliant at what she did.*

Just prior to her passing, she developed a unique sleep study, just for you. She created a platform with electromagnetic sensors built into a clear plastic domed covering, thus eliminating the need for attached sensory wiring that inhibited complete relaxation. The platform floated on water, replicating the sensation of being inside the womb, the most primordial protected environment that rendered amazing data. It was designed for your comfort and to ease any fear you may experience. It was tremendously successful in its intent.

Now, as a result of this ground- breaking study, scientists, psychologists and physicians can delve so much deeper into the phenomena of what really happens during the sleep state and better understand dimensional travel which you frequently took part in.

As for my Dad, Stephan, he's a well-known and highly respected lobbyist in Washington, D.C. who advocates for full disclosure by the United States Government regarding UFOs and the presence of what Earthlings refer to as extraterrestrials (which, I guess, would be me).

He's also demanding their acknowledgement of these phenomenon; more aptly, what is their covert agenda. Another part of his mission is to hold them accountable for the failed galactic treaties that have brought humanity and the planet to this now critical point in time...2012- the year of Prophecy!

But that's not...um...how is it referred to... oh yeah, 'the only game in town'; for there are countless ancient prophecies that are in harmony with current day scientific theories postulating what's about to happen on Earth and to her inhabitants, both above and below her surface. Yes, you heard me correctly - I said below the surface. That discussion is for another time.

Krystal suspects she's overwhelmed Bethany with all this evidence but knows she must continue:

Krystal: *Now, back to me – early on, my hybrid side appeared to be dominant, which encouraged my peers at school to tease me repeatedly. When I emerged into this physical body, I just naturally assumed that everyone else came equipped with the same...um... abilities as me; meaning they communicated telepathically, used telekinesis to move objects and could transport themselves into other dimensions at will, interact with Beings from other realities, and foretell future events.*

You, too, are charged with some of these...um...capabilities so for you and I...normal, correct?

Bethany tilts her head and shrugs her shoulders gesturing – *Ya, I guess that's what I thought so, too!*

Krystal: Well, my Dad was quick to point out that wasn't the way it was for most humans. And so, began my education in recognizing when I needed to implement limited Accelerated Human Behavior or AHB, as the psychologists referred to it. I could no longer do what came natural for me and had to consider my audience before engaging in any special action or communication. That was hard for me – really hard! To me, it was the equivalent of asking a bird not to fly.

As I was highly advanced by most scholastic standards, I was home tutored, initially. I begged my Dad to let me attend school, so I could be around other children with similar attributes. After much debate, he finally gave in and enrolled me at a private school for exceptionally 'gifted' children. That's where you and I briefly reconnected.

Unfortunately, for whatever reason, you rejected our knowing of one another, perhaps it was your desire to be more...normal than gifted. The others didn't always understand my ways and took every opportunity to taunt me about how different I was from them.

It was challenging for me to understand the way they felt, because I thought it was preferred to have these abilities; to know something was about to happen and then have it happen, exactly the way you saw it. I presume that could be unsettling, if you weren't used to it. Being able to 'hear' their thoughts really caused a lot of alienation; some called me a 'witch' or 'evil'...so, I didn't have any friends to speak of, except for you...at least for a while, anyway.

Bethany nods in complete agreement and is now more at ease and content to let Krystal prattle on with the history.

Krystal: *Okay, now I'll tell you how I came to the choosing my parents and how you were the catalyst for our first introduction. You and I first...um... 'met' before I came into human physical form...remember? At the play house.*

Because you were an exceptionally elevated psychic who was easily able to traverse between dimensions with assistance from The Keepers, as you call them, you were chosen as the perfect 'playmate' for young hybrids such as me. Since you and I had already become inter-dimensional playmates, when my Mom scheduled the sleep study with you, that offered the perfect opportunity for me to see if I could transport myself back with you to 'view' my soon-to-be chosen parents, which were Elizabeth and Stephan.

The young from all dimensions share a common universal thread with one another – they have a natural curiosity and they love to play. While it's true, what's considered 'play' varies significantly throughout the Universe. For example: Zeta Reticuli offspring enjoy dissecting smaller species. Since they lack emotion, there is no malice either expressed or intended. Their mega-minds hold an unusually high level of inquisitiveness and so need to satiate the need to evaluate and conclude the data found in their...er... 'toys.'

Bethany stifles a groan, then chuckles at this new information.

Krystal: *I know this all sounds a bit macabre, but to them it's just...play. For me, my mind is my toy; I was, and still am, able to move objects just by pure thought. Great fun, at least I thought it was, until I came into this physical reality and began showing off to my human playmates or my grandparents - believing they, too would enjoy this feat of folly, but I was totally wrong! Earth school was going to be tough - of this I was sure.*

It was mostly the older kids that messed (is that the right colloquialism 'messed'?) with me, constantly criticizing my behavior and comparing it to some old fictional TV character, Mr. Spock I believe was his name; due to my non-emotional, often verbose demeanor. I'm working on that, too.

Anyway, even though you were part of our little secret, in time you found it most difficult and couldn't handle the peer pressure any longer and so...well, you...simply broke away from me, even shunned me. I still struggle with that emotion...

Bethany lowers her head and whispers, "I'm so sorry Krystal... *truly* I am."

Not comfortable with revisiting that emotion, Krystal begins again:

Krystal: *When my Dad and I journey to Sedona each year, it's a very private time for us; one that's shared only with nature and the Universal Order. For I am told that this is exact spot where I was born. I know not all the details of my emergence as yet, but my Dad tells me that I will know all soon.*

However, he did share with me that I am considered what the Hopi tribe calls a 'Tiponi', which means 'Child of Importance.' Again, my mission is yet unclear as I speak, but know that both you and I are charged with being part of a larger plan...one that reaches far out into the galaxy.

For now, let it be enough for you to know that you have an immense role in assisting this process of renewal and transition. I'm sure you have many questions and I will attempt to answer what I can. For the ones that will remain unanswered, know this...there are many who are part of this...um...experiment and together we will find the right path to bringing humanity and the galactic neighborhood into balance, harmony and enlightenment.

With Krystal's revelations finished, at least for the moment, shockingly, Bethany remains quiet and contemplative. So much to digest. Her mind races with a myriad of questions she wants to ask but is unable to articulate them as yet. Bethany will do her best to remain uncharacteristically patient, believing that her questions will be answered in due time and that all will be made clear as to her responsibility in this paramount Universal mission.

For now, it is enough to have re-awakened and to have Krystal, once again, by her side.

LARRY'S REVEAL

*T*hrough *most of my childhood, despite all the crazy things that I've said and done (which kept my Mom in a constant state of panic and confusion), ironically, my Dad always seem to understand me and my odd behavior, on some level.*

Of course, Ryan was my one and only ally, for he, too, shared some of my more unique abilities. However, he chose to keep them hidden from everyone but me! I'm not sure even Dad knew of Ryan's special gifts, at least not outwardly. I guess because I was always so "in your face" about what I saw or heard there wasn't much doubt that I took the lion's share of attention in my household.

As close as Charlie and I were...are...he never chose to talk to me about what was going on. Now, I realize there are several years between us, and I remember Charlie always being out somewhere between sporting practices or games, or simply hanging out with his friends; but nonetheless, he had to have been aware of some of the craziness that occurred under the family roof. I'm sure his school buddies talked behind my back, as a few of them had siblings my age and you know how kids talk smack about one another, especially if you were different. Me in spades!

One thing I can state unequivocally, is that if anyone had cast negative comments about his little sister, Charlie would have handled it...his way! No fanfare, no yelling matches or even if it escalated beyond words into something more physical, he'd simply take care of it and move on...not telling anyone. Charlie was loyal and protective beyond imagination. Still is. I love him dearly for that.

Getting back to my Dad, right after one of my trips to Sedona, he picked me up at the airport alone, as Mom had to attend something at Ryan's school.

On the way home, I prattled on and on about how amazing the area was and how I always enjoy spending time with Jarred and his extended family. However, Dad seemed distant and only listened with partial attention, which was a bit unusual. One of my Dad's most endearing traits is his attentiveness whenever his children talk. He makes it his mission to stop what he's doing, no matter how busy he is, and puts his full focus on us. Pretty amazing, I'd say.

So, when I noticed how distracted he seemed, I asked him what was up. After a long pause, he looked at me and asked if I'd mind taking a little detour, so we could talk. I remember thinking, "Oh my gosh! I hope he's not going to tell me something horrible, like Mom's sick or he's sick or..." any number of life-altering turn of events.

I think I may have even blurted out "Dad, you're scaring me... is everyone Okay?" Once he assured me that it was nothing like that, I breathed a sigh of relief...at least for a moment....

(Flashback)

The clicking of the car's blinker indicates Larry's intention to exit the highway. Turning off onto a more rural road, he heads the vehicle down a small, winding dirt road that dead-ends at a large pond, near a secluded public launching area for small boats.

Larry randomly picks a non-designated parking spot, directly facing the pond. Bethany stares blankly out the front windshield at the glistening water, while several mallard ducks peacefully paddle back and forth, dipping their colorful heads beneath the water's surface in search of a meal.

Larry reaches to disengage the ignition, the car now eerily silent. Moving his driver's seat back to allow more leg room, he then pivots towards his daughter, who follows suit in her posture and is now facing him full on, eyes questioning.

"Okay, Dad...what's up?" Larry reaches across with one hand and lovingly strokes his daughter's face, then begins: "Bethany, what I'm about to share with you, must remain between us...no one...and I mean NO ONE, must know what I'm going to tell you...at least not just yet. The reason for this request will be made obvious, especially to you...for you see...I...um...er...I, too, have the same...abilities as you...always have!" Bethany's mouth is now agape and cocks her head about to speak the question that Larry has anticipated.

"I know...I know what you're about to ask me...WHY didn't I tell you this before?" Bethany raises both hands in an affirmative gesture then states with a bit of surprised anger, "Ya think? Gosh Dad, my life has been so difficult with everyone thinking I'm some kind of weirdo and now you're telling me that you've got the weirdo gene too? Or more like ... you've passed it on!"

Larry grabs both of Bethany's hands into his, leans in and locks his eyes with hers: "Bethany, when I was a young boy, I mean really young, I began ... um...er...being 'taken' by odd looking Beings. Some of them actually looked like little kids but they had these enormous heads with jet black, vacant eyes and long spindly arms, and only a few fingers. I was very scared at first, but they assured me in whatever way...they...um...could, that I was not going to be harmed.

These Beings, while frightening to me at first, became almost like playmates of sorts...I would go to this place that looked like something here on Earth with lots of toys and familiar images and all they wanted me to do was play with some smaller beings that I could only guess were their children. Sounds odd, I know, but I'm betting you understand what I'm talking about?"

Bethany's demeanor has softened and her eyes blink in acknowledgement of her father's statements.

"Bethany, I learned that our family, our bloodline, has a long history with these Beings and that they chose us...US...to be part of some inter-galactic experiment to teach their young how to interact and blend in with our species. We were the teachers... we were to show them the ways of our planet.

I also learned how this has been going on since time began, but it has accelerated in the last several decades with their presence no longer being viewed as fantasy or someone's crazy imagination. You and I both know...they are real!"

Bethany's eyes begin to well with tears, "Dad, this explains so much...so, so much...but again, why didn't you tell me...help me all those years...I struggled so much?", her voice trails off.

Larry bows his head and wipes a tear from his own eyes as he continues: "I know...honey...I know. I am so very sorry that it took me this long...but I had my reasons..." Bethany blurts out defiantly "What! What reason could you possibly have had to keep me in the dark about all this...What, Dad?"

"Bethany, please, PLEASE try to understand! When I was experiencing all this, no one else I knew, was going through the same thing and that, alone, was very intimidating. But even more so, were the threats to my life that were being made by men from the government who somehow knew that I was traveling between dimensions and teaching hybrids, HYBRIDS, Bethany! It was overwhelming! I simply knew I had to keep my mouth shut and not tell a living soul! Even as a grown man, I've not told another person, until now...you!"

Bethany's gaze leaves her father for a brief moment to stare out onto the calming waters. She takes in a deep breath and begins: "Dad, I'm doing exactly the same thing and for probably just as long as you did as a child. Ryan knows of my...um... visitations...and surprisingly has remained silent about it. In the beginning he was resentful that he couldn't go...actually, I don't know why they didn't take him as well.

Anyway, after some time, my experiences took a dark turn and I was in jeopardy from people who wanted to use me and my connections with the hybrids for their own reasons, whatever those were. Honestly Dad, I didn't want to know.

As a matter of fact, that man, that man you brought to dinner one night...what was his name...Hux...Huxley! Ya, that man came to my school and wanted me to introduce him to the hybrids...but I refused. The night he came to dinner and I took him out in the back yard to look at the garden, he grabbed my arm and insisted that we have a talk, but then, something else happened that I can't quite remember...but the next thing I knew, he was walking back into the house and asking to leave. Do you remember that night, Dad? Do you?"

Larry pauses for a moment and recalls the client but apologized for not knowing who Huxley really was. "Bethany, part of why I didn't tell you about my own experiences is because 'they' did something to my memory. It's like they erased a lot of stuff from my head, so while at some level I 'got it', consciously it was foreign to me. Does that make sense?"

Bethany nods, then shares her MILAB abduction by the military, and how they placed her on a metal table and were about to do unspeakable testing on her young body. "Dad, I was rescued...saved, actually...by one of those beings from my visits with the hybrids, only this one was big, really big...he called himself..." (in unison, Bethany and her father shout aloud) ... "The Keeper!"

"You know him, too?" Bethany shouts, wide-eyed, her voice almost shrill.

"Yes, *YES!* He's the one who watched over me and I believe he is the one who also erased my memory. But I...like you, slowly regained those memories in time but consciously chose to keep them hidden. Bethany, I needed to protect myself and my family and the only way I knew how was to deny my past...for it served no one to let my true identity to be known...especially you kids."

Larry continues, "When I first became aware of your...um... inherited talents...I was frightened beyond words for you. I prayed that you'd eventually dismiss them and that everyone else would consider them the result of an overactive imagination. But they continued...and your abilities increased with such intensity and accuracy that we couldn't ignore it any longer. What was I to do, but to discourage you and demand that you stop telling people what you 'saw' in their future. I'm sorry, Bethany (wiping a solitary tear from his eye). I truly am."

Bethany reaches out her hand to enfold her father's as a sign of understanding and forgiveness, then states softly, "Dad, you know Ryan has it, too." To which Larry whispers back... "I *know...*"

Father and daughter collapse backward into their respective car seats. Exhausted from the revelation. Bethany has so much more to share with her father about her experiences and wants to tell him more details about her time with Liz and Stephan, more importantly...Krystal! But decides...it can wait.

It is Larry who breaks the momentary silence: "Bethany, again, I just wanted you to know...that I am so sorry for not being there for you when you needed me, but know this...I am here for you now! I don't know what any of all this means, but I'm sure that we're going to find out...for you, me and now, Ryan...have been chosen!"

HERE AND NOW

*F*in$ al Thoughts:*

Well, here I am some six years later; I'm now in my mid-twenties and how drastically the world has changed (and not necessarily for the better; politically, socially, technologically, never mind geographically). It's mind blowing!

The human race is facing some of the biggest challenges in its history, for the planet is dying; from our vast oceans to the highest mountainous ranges. Mother nature put on quite a show in 2012, the year of Prophecy, just as Krystal had warned, with an increase in major violent storms, frequent earthquakes, an upsurge of melting ice caps and man's proliferation in destroying our Rain Forests. The rising seas, climate change and the continued pollution of the air that we breathe will soon reach critical mass, where nothing can be done to reverse our self-inflicted, self-destructive fate.

I don't know if you've noticed or not, but our skies are littered with toxic chemical streaks, called "Chemtrails", that run from horizon to horizon. These Chemtrails are highly visible, created in the air by spray systems onboard unmarked airplanes that fly at varying altitudes with no known purpose, at least to the masses.

Once viewed as the result of simple contrail emissions from jets that normally dissipate within minutes, these emissions differ greatly and can be seen from one end of the horizon to the other. As they fan out into the atmosphere, they merge with others in proximity forming the so-called "canopy of haze"; altering the once clear blue skies that are now awash with filmed white clouds and weather changes that almost always follow.

Independent laboratory studies report that the contents and effects from the reddish-brown gel that's being released by these Chemtrails were found to be teaming with biological organisms, such as barium and aluminum and have unusual smells and tastes, with some people reporting feeling ill when they are present in our skies.

Of course, there are plenty of theories, mostly conspiratorial, that they're part of the U.S. military's interest in weather manipulation. "Control the weather…control the world."

If it were just the United States behind this, then why are they present in the skies around the globe? I'm pretty sure that other governments wouldn't just sit back and simply allow that; unless they, too, are in partnership with a hush-hush operation, whose agenda is anyone's guess.

And yet, there are numerous countries world-wide who are finally releasing previously classified U.F.O. documentation in support of visitations from other planetary beings and some are even going so far as to acknowledge their interaction with multiple extraterrestrial species. So, you'd think they'd at least admit to the Chemtrail phenomenon, which pales in light of the release and acknowledgement of credible documentation concerning U.F.O. activity and interaction with alien beings. I can't seem to wrap my brain about that one.

As far as I know, alien abductions have slowed to a crawl, or, at the very least, perhaps not being reported as frequently as was the case during the last few decades.

There's been an amazing increase of individuals who are stepping forward and committing their lives to researching and exposing the truth relative to the U.F.O. and E.T. experiences; such as Dr. Stephen Greer, head of CSETI (Center for the Study of Extraterrestrial Intelligence) and The Disclosure Project, along with Steven Bassett, a UFO Disclosure lobbyist, like Liz's husband Stephan, along with many others who are demanding full disclosure on the government's Truth Embargo concerning this U.F.O phenomenon and their interaction with extraterrestrials.

Today, the children working within the Program to assist hybrids integrate in our earthbound world, are no longer "taken", as I once was in my early years. For it appears new methods of teleportation are allowing humans the ability to transport themselves, inter-dimensionally at will, so as to interact with their alien counterparts. But I digress.

Once my abilities reawakened, (at warp speed, I might add,) my brain was flooded, if not overwhelmed, with memories of my life since birth (actually, even before that!). In fact, I began experiencing new, or at least heightened, talents that so changed my life's direction that I'm now working with a private research facility that sought me out (I'm sure with the help of The Keeper) and now I'm one of many who work directly with hybrids and other children who display similar unique and high-level aptitudes. So, I guess you could say...the Program continues... but definitely not in the same way or manner as before.

The Keeper and I still interact, only not as often. I like to think that we've formed a sort of friendship (a term he refuses to acknowledge or accept) but nonetheless, is totally committed to me and our cooperative mission. He's proven that over and over again.

A large part of the experimentation and training with the hybrids is to help them explore their emotional human side. In my brief time with Krystal, she, too, spoke of the need to further cultivate and balance her human emotional side with her pragmatic, clinical hybrid side. This is something The Keeper cannot relate to as he is not a hybrid. And yet, every now and then I swear...

It goes without saying that the U.S. Government and others, such as the Black Ops, or the privatized covert groups like the Huxley Corporation (he may be gone, but his goons carry on his work), continue to keep a close watch on my activities and those I work alongside with. But for whatever reason, they seemed to remain strictly observant and tend to not interfere. At least that's what I intuitively interpret, but I could be wrong. I say this because I am NOT superhuman and for all I know, they could still be manipulating things behind the scenes, waiting for an opportunity to stick their nose in and take over. It's sort of like watching a spy movie, trying to figure out the good guys from the bad guys. The lines get pretty blurred on that one.

You need to remember, we're dealing with several different off-planet species of an accelerated intelligence and technology, so whatever control is assumed, is a big mistake - for the upper-hand can be gotten at any moment by any number of entities. Intriguing? – sure. Challenging and dangerous? – you bet!

Another big change is with my family. After my Dad revealed his own experiences and participation within the Program (and don't forget, brother Ryan), at Dad's insistence, we had no choice but to let Mom in on everything. That was fun. Thankfully, Dad took the lead by talking to Mom first, then gathered the entire family for a sit-down to discuss what's next.

Mom finally admitted that deep down she knew that my diagnosed "clinical, dysfunctional behavior" really was the result of something far bigger…something she deliberately chose not to accept because it was so over-the-top, and just wanted it to go away. And it did, actually, for a while; but once my memory and abilities returned, along with Ryan's blossoming hidden talents, she just couldn't deny it any more.

Now Charlie, well, that was a different story. He freaked out at first and then became livid that he couldn't do what Dad, Ryan and I could do. But Dad found the words to express how this was a 'bloodline' inheritance from his side of the family and because Charlie wasn't his biological son, etc.…well, that did the trick. I still chuckle remembering how Charlie cornered Ryan and I after our family sit-down, begging us to show him how we do what we do. Um...no can do! Sorry Charlie...doesn't work that way. I give him props for the attempt, though.

There were, however, some casualties along the way for us all. Once I began working for the research lab, try as we might to keep things under wraps, the community-at-large got wind of where I worked and while they had no real information about what we really did there, it was enough that it was regarded as one of "those" places that conducted questionable experiments.

So, one by one, a few friends and neighbors fell out of step and stopped talking to us. Sad, but that's the way people react to things they don't understand.

The good news is, since Mom and Dad had become empty nesters by then, they sold the family home and moved to a new house in a town far removed from prying eyes.

Jarred and I are still in touch with one another. I miss him terribly, but his career has gone global, so his travel schedule never seems to allow him time for any visits. I long to reunite with him, especially if we could carve out a trip to Sedona. That would make us both very happy. Jarred remains very special to me. I'm still not sure of what our future holds with one another, but I'm willing to hang in until we figure it all out.

As far as humanity-at-large, the atmosphere surrounding the 'Are they here?' mentality is long gone and it is now widely accepted, quietly and without fanfare, that they ARE here and, in some realms, welcomed and embraced.

The old fear of aliens taking over our planet and killing everyone has given way, reluctantly I will admit, to pondering the possibilities that these stellar Beings may just be looking out for our well-being, if, for no other reason, then for the sake of the planet itself...for it IS prime real estate in the galactic neighborhood.

Here's a little-known fact: There have been numerous reports of U.S. nuclear war heads unexpectedly, unexplainably and simultaneously being shut down by an unidentified source, which isn't even remotely possible, as stated by military experts and yet has happened, more than once. Those on the front lines are convinced that inter-galactic interference was the cause. So, if "They", meaning the aliens, wanted us annihilated, then they'd simply sit back and let us do their dirty work for them.

We are the hostile ones! We, in our technological infancy are a danger to ourselves...not THEM! Until we learn to play nice, we won't be allowed entrance into the galactic neighborhood, so they're keeping a watchful eye and intervene only when there is no other option.

Now, don't get me wrong, they're not ALL benevolent, heck no! There are Beings who do wish us harm and would gladly let the chips fall where they may in our de-evolution. However, and I say this reverently, thank God there are those of a more advanced evolution and benevolence that are able to keep the checks and balances, lest we destroy humanity and our beautiful planet. But there are no guarantees, so we must be vigilant and learn from previous mistakes and cultures on how to move forward and evolve.

The beauty, knowledge and insight found in so many indigenous cultures, such as the Native Americans, have much to share and to teach us, for they are the modern-day stewards of the planet.

Unfortunately, their voices have been stifled and considered non-relevant. Their anecdotes of interactions with Star Beings are ridiculed and mocked as folklore instead of being viewed as a road map of where we've come from and where we are headed. We are making a huge mistake by not listening to the elders whose wisdom is plentiful and valuable. Science and technology, alone, are no guarantee of understanding of how things work nor are they the complete formula for Earth's continuation.

We regurgitate old beliefs and information of our theoretical beginnings. We blindly follow paths that are flawed at their premise, due to the insistence of those who would have us believe they know best or, more likely, keep us dummied down for their own suspect agenda and control.

In my work with off-planet Beings, specifically the hybrids, I am in awe of their knowledge and pray for the day when it will be safe for them to reveal themselves and share the details of the Universe as they have come to know it. Like I said, there is no guarantee that simply by listening and accepting those of difference, the world would be in much better stead than it is now. But what would it hurt to give that a try?

My journey has taken a precocious, sometimes headstrong (not always to my advantage) child into adulthood and shown me things most people can't even begin to imagine, let alone comprehend. Now, as a young woman, more than ever, I am totally aware of who walks among us. You don't have to have all the psychic bells and whistles I do to notice, but don't close your mind or heart to the possibilities.

Should you encounter someone who appears a bit different, someone who seems "out of place", whether it be in their physical demeanor (moves awkwardly in their human bodies - not from an obvious impairment) or puts forth an unusual manner of speaking (monotoned, almost robotic), they just might – MIGHT be a hybrid.

I've run into many in my travels, and not just at the research facility I work for; I'm talking about them being present at the grocery store or perhaps they are posing as a waiter or a waitress serving you at a restaurant or simply walking through the park. But know this...they ARE here and they ARE blending in!

Consider this - your ancestry is so much more than where your parents, grandparents, great grandparents and great, great grandparents were born on this beautiful blue planet, for you are the by-product of the universe itself! In essence we're ALL hybrids, seeded from Galactic dust that makes up our world. We are from ALL THAT IS out there - for we possess universal DNA!

So, the next time you look at your elders, siblings, children, nieces, nephews, cousins, and even yourself in the mirror - consider these possibilities... and watch what happens!

Before I leave you, I wanted to share that it has been six years since my reconnection with Krystal, that magical day in Sedona in 2012, the Year of Prophecy. I was totally locked and loaded to take whatever action was necessary to fulfill my role in bringing our planet to its next evolutionary plane. However, sad to say, I've not seen or heard from her since that encounter and don't honestly know how or where to find her. But I refuse to give up trying.

Destiny had brought us together – so destiny will once again intervene to reunite us when the need arises, for Krystal and I have a bond that is not of this earth. It is universal, it is eternal and it is of paramount importance not only to our own soul's journey but to that of this magnificent planet we call Earth.

Krystal and I will find our way back to one another, of that I am sure, and together we will join with the others, whose mission is to help peacefully blend and unite humanity along with the benevolent Star Beings into our next universal evolution.

Final thought – What it really all comes down to is – it's up to US to make the positive changes needed so that humanity, our species, our cultures, our society, our planet, can endure. It is our birthright and duty, as members of the universal community, to do our best to keep the peace in our extraordinary diversity, nurture and show respect to the spirit of Mother Earth (our home), and to honor all living creatures, as life itself is a privilege, not an expectation.

A well-known Hopi Indian prophecy sums it up perfectly and says it all –

"WE are the ones we've been waiting for."

The world, the galaxy, the Universe - awaits our contribution!

About the Author

A former native of Boston, Massachusetts, Louise Rose Aveni has dabbled in fictional writing for many years. It wasn't until her bout with cancer in the mid 80's that she found her true literary voice. Simultaneously, as her spirit awakened, a long-time curiosity with the idea of life on other planets and inter-dimensional realms gave rise to a renewed passion to explore the possibilities in earnest.

No longer concerned with how she would be perceived in her pursuit to obtain answers to her own core questions, Louise Rose penned her first novel titled LUPO-Conversations with an E.T."; next came "HYBRID-The Conversation Continues", then finally "KRYSTAL 2012-A New Beginning", completing the HYBRID – The Trilogy saga.

And now, due to the overwhelming demand from her readers to know more about a five-year old character named Bethany, an extremely high-level psychic, intuitive and empath, who worked closely with young hybrids, teaching them the ways of our planet so that they could walk among us undetected, **CHOSEN-Bethany's Story** was created as a spin-off to the HYBRID trilogy.

"My intention for writing this trilogy and its spin-off was to put a non-threatening, benevolent face to those Star Beings who have walked among us since the beginning of recorded time and in preparation for their inevitable global contact, albeit to

eni

government's continual denial of their very

radio talk show host of "Now That's What I'm
!" via Sedona Talk Radio and Blog Talk Radio,
provided an audible vehicle to interview prominent
advocates, men and women of science, as well as
authors who shared their immense knowledge and
.ence relative to the subject of UFOs and the E.T. experience.

As an internationally published author, Louise Rose has had
the honor and privilege to speak before national audiences
on this subject along with Steven Bassett, the only registered
UFO lobbyist in the world. She has also been graced by having
world-renowned nuclear physicist, Stanton Friedman, write the
all-important Foreword to "HYBRID-The Trilogy".

Currently a resident of Sarasota, Florida, Louise Rose works
as a freelance Ghostwriter, Editor, and Marketing Consultant
and is known as "The Book Shepherd", facilitating creative
writing workshops and consultations for other aspiring authors
in their quest to write, publish, and promote their own literary
works and may be contacted at: louiseaveni@gmail.com.

And finally, Louise Rose also enjoys writing children's stories,
such as "There's an Angel in My Closet" and "SquirrelyPants
Meets the Family", co-authored by her then ten-year old
grandson, Cody. As a songwriter, she received national acclaim
for her holiday hit, "Santa, Can I Ride My Bike in Heaven?",
donating proceeds to children's cancer organizations.

All of Louise Rose Aveni's books and music are available on
Amazon.com.

CPSIA information can be obtained
at www.ICGtesting.com
Printed in the USA
LVHW090233250619
622139LV00003BA/463/P